In this together

Stories of romance and survival during the pandemic

Bella Books, Inc.
P.O. Box 10543
Tallahassee, FL 32302

This is a work of fiction. Names, characters, businesses, places, events and incidents are either the products of the author's imagination or used in a fictitious manner. Any resemblance to actual persons, living or dead, or actual events is purely coincidental. The publisher does not have any control over and does not assume any responsibility for author or third-party websites or their content.

Printed in the United States of America on acid-free paper.

First Bella Books Edition 2021

Cover Designer: Pol Robinson
Background Cover Photo by Pol Robinson

ISBN: 978-1-64247-333-9

Table of Contents

A BIG BLUE SKY

Tracey Richardson

"What are you doing?" The words were out of her mouth before Ellis Hall registered that her wife, Amy Spencer, with singular maddening focus, was tossing clothes in an open suitcase on their bed.

"You know exactly what I'm doing."

Ellis swallowed, her voice like a hinge badly in need of oil. "I-I don't think I do." *Oh god oh god oh god.*

A withering look from Amy halted any further words from Ellis. Everything about Amy was dismissive, hurtful, cruel. Which was so un-Amy-like. She was deliberate, considerate, a methodical perfectionist who was happier listening than talking—all qualities that made her one of the best damned surgeons in the province of Ontario. And made her an awfully good partner, too. But right now, she was a stranger. A rude, obnoxious stranger.

Ellis took a long, slow breath. She would not give in to her panic that Amy, for some bizarre reason, was ambushing her with a breakup. "Amy, please stop. Let's talk about this calmly, because for whatever reason you're packing a suitcase, I do not want it to—"

"It's not about what *you* want, okay? Not this time, Ellis." Amy's eyes burned with righteous indignation. Maybe even fear. Her strength—her deliberate calmness in a crisis—was immutable. But not now. Right now, Amy was not okay.

And then realization hit. Amy had gotten it into her head to move out because she was afraid she might pick up this new virus at the hospital and pass it on to Ellis or their sixteen-year-old daughter, Mia. "Oh, honey." Tears shot to the surface as Ellis considered the depth of worry and frustration that was making Amy behave this way.

Amy's chin wobbled; breaking was not in her DNA, but boy was she coming close. "I will not put you and Mia at risk. It's non-negotiable."

The fight in Ellis reasserted itself. They were a family. How dare Amy attempt to exclude her from their most important decision as a couple since moving in together? How dare Amy make unilateral decisions *this* important? "Amy, it doesn't work like that. Not in this house. You don't get to decide our lives for all of us. You can't do this. It has to be all of us agreeing. We have to decide this together."

"Jesus Christ Ellis, don't you know there's a deadly pandemic going on? Do you not understand that it's nowhere close to being under control? That we could get sick and die? I can't risk bringing it home to you and Mia. To my parents." Amy was wringing her hands, something Ellis had never seen her do before. She didn't think Amy even knew what a nervous tic was. "God! Don't you understand how hurting the people I love would absolutely destroy me? *I'm* the problem here. *I'm* the one who poses the biggest risk because of my job. Which makes it *my* decision."

"Oh, sweetheart." Ellis closed the distance between them and pulled Amy into her, clutching her tightly, running her hand softly up and down Amy's spine. It was a few minutes before she felt Amy's body relax against her. "I love you, baby. Now let's talk this out. Calmly. Please?"

Ellis had been afraid this would happen, that Amy would follow the lead of other frontline healthcare workers and stay away from their families, their homes, out of fear of transmission. COVID-19 was out in the community, its spread expedited by migrant workers who'd recently arrived for spring planting in the fields. It was so new, testing so inadequate, that they had no idea exactly how prevalent it was in the community. Ellis had begun working from home as soon the province announced the lockdown eleven days ago, and Mia was home schooling. It was true that Amy's job posed the biggest threat to them all, but nobody was safe against this invisible enemy. They could take every safeguard in the world. Would it ultimately matter? Was there a right decision?

Their shoulders touching as they moved to sit side by side on the bed, Ellis threaded her fingers into Amy's. The ragged intake of breath made it clear Amy was every bit as close to tears as Ellis was. Maybe if they sat like this for a while, they could vanquish this nightmare out of sheer desire or insistence or, hell, even deniability. Anything to make it go away for a little while.

From the window Ellis could see clouds scudding by, the sun dipping beneath them before bursting blindingly and dazzlingly free. The sky and the lake beyond the horizon—they were the same calm blue, untouched by sickness and death. Yes, she could close her eyes and imagine everything exactly as it was three or four weeks ago. Before...*this*. She squeezed Amy's hand. She would appeal to her practical side. "Look, we'll continue to make sure your parents are cared for. We've got all their deliveries set up, we've got home care workers attending to them twice a week, we'll FaceTime them every day. Mia is happy to keep spending an afternoon a week doing chores for them. Your parents are fine. You're not going to give them this disease, okay? And Mia and I are strong, we're healthy."

Amy nodded after a moment. "I know all that. In my head, at least. But I worry."

"So do I. Especially about you."

Truth was, Ellis worried about it all. Everything. But giving into her fears…would it only make things worse? Or was she being naïve? Nobody knew where this was heading, what to do and what not to do. *What if I am doing the wrong thing by persuading Amy to stay? Do I even know what the right answer is?*

"Look. I'm fine," Amy muttered. But her usually pearl-gray eyes were charcoal dark, and the new frown permanently etched on her forehead told a different story. She was working fourteen-hour days at the hospital. With all surgeries except life-saving ones canceled, she was mostly taking shifts in the ICU, and filling in anywhere else she was needed. Sleep was rare, or any kind of rest. What concerned Ellis the most was the knot of worries, the incredible sense of responsibility Amy must be carrying inside herself. The medical profession had never been under siege like this before.

Ellis kissed their joined hands. "All I ask is that you stay here, with Mia and me. That's it. I'll look after everything else on the home front. But I need you here, even if it's only a few hours a night. You can sleep in the spare room if that makes you feel better, but please, just stay here. With us. Even if it's the wrong damned thing to do."

Amy sighed loudly, but it sounded like relief, not frustration. "I know I'm being a shitty partner right now. I'm sorry."

"You're not. You never are. And I'm okay with coming second right now, really I am. Just don't shut me out." A sob of tears clogged Ellis's throat. "I need you, Amy, and I think you need me too. We *have* to do this together."

Amy turned to Ellis and buried her head against her neck. Her voice ragged, she whispered, "I think I need you more than I've ever needed you."

"Then it's settled," Ellis replied, planting a tender kiss on her lover's lips. "You're not temporarily moving out. You're going to keep coming in the back door and throwing your clothes in the washing machine and spraying down your shoes and stuff and then showering before you see Mia or me. All right?"

After a moment, Amy nodded. "Please keep being my rock, baby."

"I will. Because you're my rock, too."

They sat for a long time together, just breathing.

* * *

The world seemed to be moving too quickly for Amy to keep her feet, and she stumbled momentarily as she entered the hospital through the staff door. The sun was waking the earth, stretching pink across the sky. A beautiful morning. A morning blissfully ignorant of deadly pandemics.

Would she even be doing this if she hadn't grown up the daughter of a physician? As a kid she'd loved her father's medical bag, its leather so soft and supple beneath her fingers. Even more, she loved the contents of the bag, would get into trouble for taking inventory and using the tools on her dolls or the family pet. Her first real stethoscope arrived in a Christmas stocking when she was ten. She took it everywhere, kept it under her pillow at night like prayer beads. Nah, she thought now, she would have become a doctor no matter what.

Her best friend Kate Henderson greeted her inside and they began the process of donning protective equipment in the sealed off, designated room for staff. Staff donned and doffed in pairs so that no steps were missed. "Any sleep last night?" Kate asked in a tone that said she already knew the answer.

"Not much."

Kate's smile was water thin. "Same here. How did Ellis take the news that you want to move out for a few weeks?"

"Not well. How about Erin?"

Amy and Kate had hatched a plan a few days ago to rent a two-bedroom apartment together for at least a month, maybe more, to keep their families safe. They both had family to protect. Amy had her elderly parents and Ellis and Mia to worry about while Kate had her new wife, Erin, a family physician in town, and Erin's young daughter, Eliana, to keep safe.

Kate shook her head. "No dice. She said we're going to get through this together, no matter what."

They all were, Amy thought. Everyone in the world, united by a virus they didn't have the tools to stop. And yet, that was where the unity ended. Every country, every region of every country, had its own ideas on how to manage the virus, none of them all that successful. Where and how and when it was all going to end remained anybody's guess.

Amy asked simply, "Can you live with *no matter what?*"

Kate shrugged as Amy tied her gown tightly behind her. "I think I'm going to have to."

They wouldn't know if they'd made the right decision to stay with their families until it was possibly too late. If she made Ellis or Mia sick, Amy thought, she'd have to deal with the guilt then, but not before. There was no longer the luxury of mulling decisions and considering every angle, trying to predict the future. Decisions these days came as swiftly as a guillotine's blade.

"Then it's done," Amy said as Kate returned the favor and tied her protective gown behind her back. "We're staying the course. But for the record, it worries me."

A whoosh of outside noise as the door opened and closed. It was Ruth Donegal, an OB-GYN. "Hey do you guys have time to watch me doff?"

"Of course," Kate replied. Kate, typically a surgical scrub nurse, had been moved to the ER two weeks ago. Ruth was one of the few staffers who hadn't been reassigned.

Ruth removed her gloves and tossed them in a sealed container that would later be headed to the hospital incinerator. "You two seeing less COVID yet?"

Kate chewed on her lower lip. "Maybe. A bit less than a few days ago, I'd say."

"The hospital census is down a fraction," Amy replied. "Some are getting better. And then there are the celestial discharges." Three deaths in the last six days, which was a lot for a hospital of fifty-eight beds serving a community of about 50,000 people. "How's it going with you?"

Ruth untied her gown, tossed it in the large bio-waste container as well. "Babies don't care what world they're being born into. COVID or no COVID, ready or not, they're coming. All I can do is keep catching them."

There was something reassuring about those who jumped and those who caught them, Amy thought. She fixed her respirator mask to her face, secured it tightly. Next was a pair of goggles, then her face shield. Gloves were last. It was a routine that had to be done exactly the same way, every single time. "Well, I'm off to the ICU, ladies. Stay safe today."

Taking the stairs up a level, Amy thought about babies being caught. She wouldn't be catching anyone in the ICU but she might be able to do some holding—vital signs, hands, hope if necessary. She'd never felt so helpless as a physician. Oxygen and steroids were her tools now, which, for a surgeon, was like calling sticks and stones weapons of war. Better than nothing, but…

Amy greeted the nurses and learned there'd been a new ICU COVID admission late last night—a woman in her early sixties. Amy scanned her patient's electronic chart. She was a grocery store worker, a volunteer at her church, widowed with a grown daughter who lived on the other side of the country. Elaine Phillips had no other underlying health conditions, but she'd been admitted with a high fever and oxygen levels trending dangerously down.

"Hello Mrs. Phillips." Amy smiled beneath her mask. She kept forgetting that people couldn't see whether she was smiling or not. "I'm Dr. Spencer and we're going to try to help you get better, okay?"

The woman nodded weakly. Her eyes had that faded, watery look of the fevered or the dying or the very old. An oxygen cannula was strapped around her face, but she would need to be put on a ventilator soon, Amy knew. Likely within hours.

Amy moved to stand closer to the bed, the beeps and rumblings of the machines reminding her that she wasn't in an OR. Operating rooms seemed almost quiet in comparison with intensive care rooms. All of this was so strange still. She was gowned and geared up as though she were working in a nuclear plant. It was damned hot and scratchy under all the PPE.

Amy tended to be frank with her patients, and Mrs. Phillips was no exception.

"Mrs. Phillips, you're—"

A hand lifted weakly off the bed in protest. "Elaine," the woman whispered.

"All right. Elaine." Amy paused to be sure she was locking eyes with her patient, since it was the only part of her face with which to express confidence, reassurance, empathy. "Your vitals have been worsening. Your last X-ray shows a lot of COVID in your lungs. The supplemental oxygen we've been giving you is not enough to raise your saturation levels. It means we're going to have to sedate you and put you on a ventilator soon. Probably by this afternoon."

The woman's eyes understandably widened in fear. It was common knowledge that a ventilator was the final act of desperation, the last tool in the tool kit while the patient's immune system tried to fight off the disease.

She stared at Amy with eyes that now held only the desire for truth. "Am I going to die?"

Oh how Amy hated when patients asked her that question, and yet, what other question could be more pressing, more important, more worthy of the truth? Amy wasn't God, she never knew with absolute certainty that a patient was going to die until their body began irretrievably shutting down. Then the answer was easy.

"I don't know…Elaine. This…disease is so new, we have no way of knowing what your chances of surviving it may be at this point. But you should prepare for…" Amy had to clear her throat, "the possibility that you may not survive it."

"Thank you," Mrs. Phillips said haltingly. "For…telling me…the truth."

All the years of pre-med, medical school, residency—none of it had prepared Amy for being so helpless in the face of a dying patient. She wanted, needed to do something. "Is there someone I can connect you with on an iPad or phone? Can I bring you something, anything?"

The woman didn't answer for a while, just stared at the window with its blinds half closed.

"Would you like to look out the window?"

"Yes. Please. If this...is the last...thing I get to look at...then I just want to...look at that big blue sky...for as long...as I can."

Amy opened the blinds all the way. Then she carefully tilted the bed to give her patient a clearer view. "Anything else I can do for you?"

"Yes. Will you sit here and...watch the sky with me?"

"Absolutely. For as long as you want." Amy pulled a chair closer to the window and sat down. There was no need to talk. Or even to think. She decided to remember, always, this shade of cerulean blue that was streaked with wisps of thin, almost gauze-like clouds. A bird, then another one, circled joyously, riding the air currents like it was a game.

It was a good day to be alive.

The characters in this short story first appeared in the novel Thursday Afternoons *by Tracey Richardson.* Thursday Afternoons *is available from Bella Books or your favorite retailer.*

MILES FROM HOME

Kat Jackson

MARCH

Monday

"*Reports from Europe indicate that Italy is seeing a dramatic increase in COVID-19 cases. In response, the Prime Minister has enforced a country-wide lockdown. Travel is permitted only for...*"

Three bitten nails later, Emery reached for the remote and pressed until she found a different national news station. She rubbed her eyes and leaned forward, already tired of staring at the TV, weary of hoping for better news.

"*We are now receiving notice that airlines are preemptively canceling and rerouting flights.*" The woman on the screen, wearing a harsh red shirt that clashed with her offensively bright blond hair, had the grace to keep a serious expression on her heavily made-up face. "*Airports in Europe have become holding tanks for American travelers trying to get home.*"

"What?" Emery said softly. "No. No, no, no."

The newscaster continued talking, but Emery couldn't take in any more of her words. She watched her mouth move and imagined her saying, "But don't worry, Emery. Burke's flight isn't canceled. She'll be back home to you soon."

Emery was so distracted by the woman and her hypnotic mouth that she missed the first incoming call to her phone. The second round of vibrations got her attention and she lunged across the room, answering just before it went to voice mail.

"Em? Are you okay? What's going on there?" Allison's frantic voice echoed in the apartment.

After sinking to the worn hardwood floor of the living room, Emery nodded and pressed the phone to her ear. "I'm okay. I think so, anyway." She pressed her palm to her forehead. "No, actually, I think I'm freaking out."

"Are you alone?"

"Of course I'm alone. Burke's still in Germany."

Allison huffed. "While I know I am forever your best friend, I'm not stupid. I know you guys have made fancy New York friends. And I'm pretty sure one of them lives in your building."

"Our friends aren't 'fancy,'" Emery said, a smile slipping onto her lips despite her internal panic. "They're normal people. Arguably more normal than you, honestly."

"That's not too difficult to achieve." Allison laughed heartily. The sound of an espresso machine whirring to life was muffled in the background.

"Wait a minute. Are you at work? I thought you were mandated to shut it down."

"Not yet. I'm worried that's coming, but for now, I need to keep this place open." Allison paused, then in a much quieter voice said, "I can't even think about what I'll do if we have to close." She cleared her throat. "What about you? Are you working from home?"

"Unfortunately, no. I was in the office all day."

"Please tell me you're not riding the subway."

"Oh, no. I'm not. I'm too freaked out to do that, plus we got some guidelines over the weekend to try to avoid subways and buses." Emery sighed as she toyed with the ripped edges of her jeans. "I can't get a hold of Burke."

"What? What do you mean?"

"I mean what I said. She hasn't answered any of my calls today. And she's not texting back, either."

"Em, I'm sure she's just busy. This was a major trip for her, wasn't it?"

"Yes. Very major. I know she's fine, and busy, like you said. It's just that...with everything going on, I wish she'd call me back."

"And I have no doubt that she will." Allison yelled something about a milk order before coming back to the conversation. "Hey, Em, I've gotta go. There's a cinnamon spill behind the counter."

"Sounds dangerous. Call me tomorrow?"

"You got it."

After double checking to make sure she didn't somehow miss a call or a text, or even an email while talking with her best friend back in Portland, Emery put her phone back down where it had been charging, then stood and crossed the room to gaze out one of the oversized windows.

Brooklyn, and Cobble Hill in particular, wasn't as bustling as Emery had thought it would be. And now, with the rapidly increasing cases of this mysterious and deadly disease, the streets were even quieter. A few people were walking down Congress Street as the sun began to set, but it was noticeably fewer than just a few days ago.

Emery tugged the sleeves of her sweater over her hands and wrapped her arms around herself. Of all the times for Burke to travel overseas, she thought. *Excellent timing.*

But of course: their timing had been terrible from the start.

About eight months had passed since Emery and Burke had packed up their lives in Portland and moved across the country to start fresh in New York. It was an easy decision to make on multiple levels: Burke got an amazing job offer in Brooklyn, Emery's promotion allowed her to transfer to the New York offices, and after taking two years to wade through the lingering complications of their new relationship, they were ready for a clean slate in a new place.

As Burke liked to tell Emery: "It took me one year to trust you, another year to let myself believe what we have is real, and one move clear across the country to fully understand how much we love each other."

None of it had been easy. Emery had known from the start how devoted she was to Burke, but considering her shady actions, she couldn't blame Burke for needing to take it slow at first. (That hadn't lasted long.) Burke was generous, open, and nervous about trusting Emery. The rightful lack of trust had nearly destroyed their relationship before it truly began, but it was Burke's best friend, Aubrey, who'd suggested they check in with a therapist. "For maintenance," she'd said.

Six months of therapy had done the trick: armed with better communication skills and an awareness of each other's feelings, regrets, and growing trust, Emery and Burke had found themselves moving forward faster than they'd planned. It was Burke's suggestion that they move in together about a year into their relationship. Emery hadn't been in a rush, but considering they were spending six out of seven nights together per week, it didn't make much sense to continue living separately.

Naturally, living together had brought its own bumps and surprises. Just when they'd gotten the hang of that, Burke's connections in New York had called, practically begging her to finally accept the tech firm job they offered her every year or so. Having grown tired of the same old scene in Portland, Emery was ready for change and put in for a transfer to PLAC's New York office.

And so, here they were: living in a two-bedroom, third-floor walk-up in Cobble Hill. The apartment itself was beautiful—slightly beat up hardwood floors, giant windows with black trim, an old brick wall in the bedroom, a spectacular original fireplace (since converted to gas), a claw-foot tub that was the envy of everyone Emery FaceTimed—and they'd taken pride in decorating it. The living room windows looked out onto Congress Street and Cobble Hill Park. They had shared access to a patio in the garden, but they also had a little deck attached to the kitchen with just enough space for two chairs and a small table.

That tiny deck had been one of the biggest selling points for Burke. When they toured the apartment, she'd stood behind Emery and held her in her arms, nuzzling her neck.

"We'll spend all our evenings on that deck, talking about our days."

Emery had shivered. "Maybe only when it's above 60 degrees?"

Burke had laughed and kissed Emery's cheek. "Pack blankets."

Friday

"I feel like I'm watching the world end, and all I can do is sit here and watch the drama surge on MSNBC."

"Babe, if it's that bad, change the channel."

"I can't! I feel like I need to stay as informed as possible."

Burke's sigh, from over three thousand miles away, was loud enough to seem like she was in the same room with Emery. "It sounds like you're informed enough. Change the channel. You need a palate cleanser or you'll never sleep tonight."

She was right, and Emery knew it. She smiled in the growing darkness of the room. "It's only seven o'clock."

"Yes, well, it's one a.m. here." She yawned. "I can't believe I'm still awake."

"I can't believe you're still in Germany," Emery said, displeasure evident in her voice.

"You know it's out of my control." Burke shifted, sending the rustle of sheets over the phone. When Emery closed her eyes, she could almost pretend they were together, snuggled under the down comforter in their cozy bedroom. "I'm doing my best to get home to you. This whole flight thing is extremely frustrating."

Emery kept her eyes shut. "Any updates on that?"

"None you'll like."

She sighed and opened her eyes. "I hate this."

"I know, my love. I do too. Hey, have you seen Lea?"

"Yup, I dropped off breakfast for her this morning. She's making me dinner tomorrow night." Their downstairs neighbor was a sweet 57-year-old widow who had taken it upon herself to be a motherly figure to Emery and Burke. Her cooking and baking skills were out of this world, so neither complained.

"Oh, good. How did she take the Broadway closure news?"

"Not well at all. You know how much she loves her plays."

Burke laughed. "Lucky for her, you can perform your one-woman show of *RENT* on demand until Broadway opens again." Another yawn came through the phone, this one louder and longer. "Emery, I'm beat. I've got an early morning of searching for flights ahead of me."

"Okay," Emery said softly. "I miss you so much."

"And I miss you. I love you."

"I love you, Burke."

The quiet fell over Emery when she hung up. She missed Burke acutely, and wasn't used to being away from her for this long. She curled up on the sofa and stared at the TV. Burke was right: she needed a palate cleanser. A couple button pushes later, an opening scene for *Broadchurch* began and the haunting pressure from the news faded away.

Sunday

The weather was doing that weird thing where it looked warm but was actually uncomfortably damp and cool. Emery pulled her jacket tighter around her body as she picked up her pace. She made sure to keep her distance from the few other people on the sidewalk, but she worried they all had the same idea in mind.

Sure enough, when she rounded the corner and spotted the entrance to the grocery store, she groaned. A line snaked out the door, and people stood, shifting eyes and feet. A strange silence hung over the group.

Emery took her place at the end of the line. She stuffed her hands in her pockets and buried her chin in her sweatshirt. She wouldn't call herself paranoid, exactly, but the news reports coming in at all hours of the day weren't helping the nagging unsafe feeling she had.

Sensing that this wait was going to drive her crazy if she remained in her head, she paused her music and hit Allison's name. A little West Coast entertainment would certainly cheer her up while she waited.

"You have incredible timing," Allison said as she answered the phone. "I just got into Perk and I'm freaking the fuck out because there are no customers. Zero. Absolutely none."

"Isn't it kind of early?" Emery glanced at her phone. "Since when do you open at six a.m. on a Sunday?"

"Em, I have no choice right now. I need to make as much money as possible." The panic in Allison's voice hurt Emery's heart; this wasn't a common sound from her friend. "I already temporarily laid off two of my baristas."

"Well, if it goes to bust, you can always drive here and hang out with me!" Emery tried for cheery but missed the mark.

"Um, right, because it's a smart idea to travel somewhere where people are packed into small spaces all the time. No thanks. Besides, didn't you just tell me yesterday that people are *leaving* the city?"

"Yeah. My upstairs neighbors packed up and headed to their in-laws upstate. They said it's an 'extended weekend,' but considering they were both already told to work from home, I don't think they'll be back anytime soon."

"Wild," Allison muttered. "How are you holding up? Are you working from home yet?"

"No," Emery said slowly. "I'm still going into the office. Since I can walk there, it doesn't feel like a big deal, plus I'm usually by myself unless we have a meeting." And since her boss had canceled every meeting for the last two weeks, Emery had been by herself a bit too much. She dropped her voice. "I'm waiting in a long line to get into the grocery store."

"Oh boy. The real panic has set in, huh?"

"Can you blame me? Who knows what's going to happen next?"

"Yeah, I hear you. For once, I don't think you're overreacting."

"How kind of you," Emery said dryly as she moved up several paces. "I don't even know what to buy."

"What do you East Coast people buy when a storm's coming? Milk, butter, and eggs, right?"

"Yeah, because making french toast during a blizzard is a top priority." Emery laughed. "I'm thinking I need more practical standards for this kind of storm."

"Make sure you grab bananas."

Emery wrinkled her nose. "Gross. Not a fan. Why?"

"To make banana bread. Duh."

Emery shook her head, not understanding Allison's logic. But she'd grab bananas anyway, just in case. "Okay. I need to concentrate and make a plan. I'll call you later."

"Don't forget the bananas! And maybe stuff for a sourdough starter, if you can find it!"

After ending the call, Emery stared at her phone in confusion. When did Allison start believing Emery was some kind of master baker?

Navigating the grocery store had been a lesson in patience, determination, and a test of Emery's foraging skills. She emerged mostly unscathed but ready to get the hell home and not have to leave her apartment again.

The sun had dipped behind a thick line of clouds and the air had cooled while she was inside. Despite being loaded down with several heavy bags of pantry standards, Emery walked quickly. More people were out now, most heading toward the same store Emery had left. She was thankful for her quick thinking earlier that morning; this was normally the kind of thing Burke would decide to do, but in her absence, practicality fell onto Emery's plate.

Her heart sank a bit as she turned onto Congress Street. The ache of missing Burke was a weight that increased each day. They hadn't spent much time apart since they'd moved in together back in Portland, and this was the first time Burke's job had taken her overseas. They both knew that was going to be part of the gig, and under normal circumstances, Emery assumed she'd handle it better.

Lugging bags of groceries up three flights of stairs was by far Emery's least favorite thing about their apartment. By the time she got to their door, she was breathing heavily and cursing their poor apartment choices. She fumbled with her keys, finally finding the right combination, and shoved her shoulder against the door.

Her nose perked immediately to the smell of coffee. Not just any coffee: the luxurious breakfast blend from Burke's favorite coffee shop on Court Street. She wrinkled her forehead in confusion. *How…what?* She definitely hadn't gotten coffee that morning; she'd been too consumed with her grocery store plan of attack.

Then her eyes spotted the suitcase sitting by the front door. It took every bit of Emery's strength to hang on to her grocery bags as she bolted into the kitchen.

"Well, hello there, beautiful."

Once in the entryway to the kitchen, Emery unceremoniously dropped the groceries and threw herself into Burke's open arms.

APRIL

Tuesday

Emery rolled over and wrapped her body around Burke's. She was greeted with a grunt, one she'd become familiar with after they'd moved in together. She'd foolishly thought Burke would like mornings more when they continuously woke up side by side, but no, it turned out that Burke's loathing for mornings was a lifelong conflict that would never be resolved.

"Five more minutes," followed the grunt.

"More like two. You slept through both alarms again."

Another grunt, this one slightly more lethal sounding, emerged. Burke sleepily grabbed Emery's hand and tugged her closer and tighter. "You can take my meetings today."

"Oh, no, that's not happening. We may be stuck working in the same office now, but honey, I've got my own meetings to attend."

The "office," of course, was their living room. They took turns using the second bedroom, which was mostly a storage room with a full-sized bed, when they needed privacy or a quieter environment for calls or online meetings. Burke had rearranged the items in the room to create an aesthetically pleasing nook that provided an uncluttered background for their Google Meets.

Emery poked Burke in the side, hard enough to serve as a warning, before getting out of bed and padding into the kitchen. The only way to rouse Burke from her bed-cocoon was with the alluring scent of freshly brewed coffee. And since the entire city was shut down, Emery had to make the coffee herself. Burke humored her, saying it was just as good as her favorite brews from the café on Court Street, but Emery saw right through her smoke and mirrors.

While she waited for the coffee to percolate, Emery opened her laptop and scanned her calendar. It was a lighter day—the lightest of the week—with only one virtual meeting. The rest of the day was hers to work on reports and check in, via email or phone calls, with her team. When all non-essential workers were instructed to work from home, Emery's project with a local business had stalled. It was borderline impossible to consult with a company through online-only interactions, but they were making the best of it. Emery was finding that she liked having to come up with new ideas to fit the current situation, sometimes with only an hour to spare.

A shuffling sound echoed down the hallway and soon, Burke appeared in the kitchen, her hair adorably rumpled (and a bit longer than usual since she couldn't get in for her monthly cuts), eyes half-mast. She went about fixing her coffee, a task she still refused to let Emery handle, and after three full-mouthed sips, she put her mug down and reached for Emery.

"Why is it so much harder to get up and go to work when your living room is your office?" she mumbled into Emery's hair.

"Because we no longer have that very necessary separation between work and home." Emery stroked Burke's back. "But I don't hear you complaining about the ability to make out with your coworker whenever you feel like it."

Burke pressed her lips against Emery's head. "Maybe we should push our luck and try for a lunchtime quickie today. I heard there's a bed in the employee break room."

"I like the sound of that. Want me to send you some sexy selfies from the women's bathroom while you're on your 9 a.m. meeting?"

"Only if you're wearing something lace and vaguely transparent."

"Your wish," Emery said, pulling back to kiss Burke's lips, "is my command."

Thursday

It seemed that with each passing minute, Burke's voice was getting louder. It couldn't be possible, Emery reasoned, because Burke was so damn even-tempered that she didn't even *raise* her voice to begin with. But, no, she swore she was bumping up the decibel level every time she spoke.

With a frustrated growl, Emery got up from the sofa and crept down the hall, looking to make sure the door to the spare bedroom was shut. It was. She wrinkled her forehead in confusion, then jumped back as Burke's voice boomed through the thin door once again.

"What is her *problem*?" Emery hissed to the empty hallway. She hovered at the door, debating whether or not she should knock gently and ask sweetly if her darling girlfriend could please, pretty please, talk a little more quietly. She had a virtual meeting starting in five minutes, a really important one with a handful of very sensitive people, and the last thing she needed was for Burke's new thunderous voice to interrupt her session on communication.

When Burke spoke again, it was at normal volume, and Emery returned to her laptop, hoping she would stay at that volume. Perhaps she should have hoped that Burke would stay in their makeshift office.

Not ten minutes into Emery's session, Burke blasted out of the room, talking loudly and animatedly on her phone. Emery gestured wildly at her, but she didn't see her. Shifting her gaze between her computer and her bizarrely loud girlfriend, Emery waited for Burke to leave.

Oh, no, she didn't leave. Burke apparently needed to *pace*, and pace she did, traveling up and down the hallway, through the living room and combined dining area of their apartment. As she paced, she continued to talk, her free arm moving spasmodically when she hit a really exciting idea.

Meanwhile, Emery was waiting for Zadie, the lovely head of finances at Hardy and Miller, Inc., to finish her long-winded hypothesis about company revenue so she could pause the meeting and slip into the "office" to finish her session in moderate peace. She was distracted by Burke's uncharacteristic behavior, and she missed the point in which Zadie paused to let Janeya jump in.

"That's fantastic!" Burke yelled, her voice jumping back from every corner of the room. Emery flinched and sure enough, her on-screen participants stopped talking and peered at her with curiosity.

"I'm so sorry," Emery said hurriedly. She grabbed her laptop, pulling it clean from its charger, and hurried into the abandoned bedroom. "Just a miscommunication here in the home office." She sat down and repositioned her laptop, fixing a happy, caring smile on her face. "Janeya, you were saying?"

A half hour later, Burke poked her head into the room, a sheepish look warming her features. She was greeted with an icy glare, icicle-daggers shooting from across the room. She disappeared as quickly as she'd appeared.

Emery was again listening to Zadie belabor one of her many grievances when her phone buzzed on the desk.

Hey, cutie down the hall. I heard you're having a bad day. Any chance I can buy you a cup of coffee at the vending machine in an hour?

While maintaining her virtual composure, Emery jabbed out a response.

Not happening. My new coworker (AKA YOU) is the reason for my bad day. Find someone else to bother with your lame vending machine coffee.

Undeterred, Burke replied within seconds.

Ouch. Well, I'll be here all day…and all night…also tomorrow… and every foreseeable day thereafter…if you change your mind. And I hope you do. xo

UNLIKELY. After hitting send, Emery pushed her phone away and concentrated on her clients.

Sunday

The fresh air felt like the best gift anyone had ever gifted. Emery inhaled deeply, taking in hints of spring and the still-far-off taste of summer. The end of her fulfilling inhale was snagged by the cotton fabric of her mask sealing itself to her nostrils.

"I still can't believe we got that deal with the company in Ireland," Burke said, the wonder evident in her voice. "Unbelievable."

"You worked really hard for it, babe. Especially last week." Emery shot one final glare at her.

"And I've promised I'll be a more considerate coworker from now on."

"And?"

"And," Burke continued, her smile showing in her eyes, "if I ever need to excitedly pace again, I will take it outside."

"Thank you."

"You know…"

Emery side-eyed her, not liking the sound of that. "Burke? Is your following statement going to disrupt this beautiful day and our masked stroll through our reasonably safe neighborhood?"

"Yes and no." Burke squeezed her hand. "This won't happen for a while, not until it's safe to travel overseas again, but I'm going to have to go to Ireland. Probably for a while."

Emery's heart bottomed out. Burke had told her that this new job would involve traveling overseas, and Emery was fine with that—but after Burke getting stuck in Germany when Emery needed her most here in Brooklyn, she didn't love the idea of her traveling again.

"Define 'a while.'"

"Possibly a month. It really shouldn't be longer than that."

Emery sighed, the fabric of her mask again assaulting her breathing orifices. "Can you please try to arrange this trip so that it doesn't fall in the middle of a global pandemic?"

"I'll do my best." Burke swung their clasped hands. "Anything for you."

Later that night, Emery and Burke sat on their sofa, staring happily at the array of Indian food on their coffee table.

"I'm so relieved we can get takeout," Emery said before stuffing a torn piece of naan into her mouth. "No offense, but I was getting tired of your cooking."

"Excuse me. I happen to know I'm a talented chef."

"You're a great cook, yes. But you make the same four things over and over again." Emery cringed. "I didn't think I'd ever say this, but I am so sick of black bean tacos."

"Life would be better if we had a grill." Burke perked up. "Wait! We have room for a small grill on the deck, don't we?"

Emery looked toward the rear of the apartment. "I think we do. Shall we order one tomorrow?"

"We shall." Burke leaned over and kissed Emery, holding her chin gently as their lips moved together. When she pulled away, she left just an inch between them, her caramel-colored eyes locked with Emery's. "Thank you."

Emery smiled shyly. "What are you thanking me for?"

"Being you. Doing this with me. Trusting me with your heart."

"I love you so much," Emery whispered, brushing her lips against Burke's. "You're the only person I'd want to be stuck with like this."

"Even when I'm a bad coworker and accidentally drive you crazy?"

Emery laughed. "It's funny; technically we worked together years ago, but I had no idea your work personality is so... big."

"A lady has to keep some secrets." Burke winked and kissed Emery once more.

"That's a secret you can keep." Emery grinned at Burke's feigned hurt expression. "But just so you know, even though I'm not the biggest fan of your loud work personality, I still adore you."

"You better." Burke dipped her chunk of naan into the mango chutney she refused to share. "Hey. Since we're working late tonight…"

Emery glanced around. "Looks like everyone went home early."

"Maybe we could check out that break room bed later."

"If you're lucky," Emery said.

"Oh, I'm already lucky. I'd like to get a little luckier, if you know what I mean."

Emery laughed and shook her head. "Terrible. Absolutely terrible."

"You love it."

With a broad smile, Emery nodded. "More than you'll ever know."

The characters in this short story first appeared in the novel Begin Again *by Kat Jackson.* Begin Again *is available from Bella Books or your favorite retailer.*

WE WILL REVEL IN THE CROWD

Ann Roberts

Once again, we will revel in the crowd.

Spontaneity will step off the sideline.
We'll take a drive to the coast,
Bring a gift to a friend in need,
Help a neighbor with an *indoor* project.

And sociology will sigh in contentment.

Once again, we will revel in the crowd.

We will usher in anticipation, excitement, and desire.
We'll leap from our seats at the swish of a 3-pointer,
Applaud madly at the curtain call of a musical we've longed to
    see,
Hover with our besties around the TV, our faces full of awe,
    until Simone Biles sticks the landing and collects her gold.

Once again, we will revel in the crowd.

The electricity of connectivity will reignite us.
Social distancing signs will disappear.
Waiting outside a favorite venue, shoulder to shoulder,
An accidental bump evokes an "Oh, I'm so sorry," and instead
   of a glare, the offender is met with "oh, you're ok."

Once again, we will revel in the crowd.

The First Amendment will awaken safely.
We'll link arms, walk forward together, marching, protesting,
   chanting, our respiratory droplets united for a cause.

We will huddle in solitude,
Heads bowed, hands clasped, voices barely a whisper,
Finally mourning those we lost, their honor postponed.
We'll comfort those whose feelings have hung in suspension,
Crying, laughing and celebrating the glorious lives of those
   we've known.

Once again, we will revel in the crowd.

We will "i-n-g" the hell out of life
Flinging graduation mortarboards,
Releasing matrimonial doves,
Clapping crazily for great performances,
Paddling the river,
Singing together
Dancing, picknicking, hiking, wine tasting, romancing,
   praying, touching,
Basking in the sounds of joy.

We will turn this page.
Silence will cease to be the norm.
Loneliness and being alone will no longer be synonymous.
We will meet our highly resilient children again as they
   emerge from hibernation.

Board games, puzzles, and books returned to closet shelves, but
    maybe not so high a shelf.
We'll forget our Zoom passwords,
Toss our K-95 masks into drawers or gloveboxes,
Exchanging them for our more customary, comfortable and
    public masks.

Moving forward with a much greater appreciation than we
    could ever articulate to future generations.
Because
We wouldn't,
We couldn't,
We didn't.

Once again we will revel in the crowd.

The weekend will complete the sentence of our work.
Birthdays, Barbeques, Happy Hours, Movies and Dinners
We'll gladly drop our money on the bar,
Generously tip the gig workers still coming back from the
    brink,
And nurture the fragile economies and emotions of our
    neighbors.

Soon, soon. We will revel in the crowd.

SO CLOSE TO HOME

RJ Layer

Lauren pulled in under the carport, swung her legs out of her car and leaned down to loosen her shoelaces. Inside the laundry room she plopped her purse and bag on the dryer, then stripped off her scrubs and everything sans panties, dropping them in the washer with yesterday's work clothes. The sixth twelve-hour shift in as many days had her dead on her feet. Everything ached but her hair. Anticipating two days off, she grabbed her robe from the door and crept through the house to the bathroom without waking Van where she snoozed in her recliner. Van's day had probably consisted of running an end loader for eight long hours for Cornett Construction.

She relaxed as the shower spray warmed, allowing the water to slide over her pinkening skin and carry her day's stress down the drain. A few minutes later she felt Van's presence before seeing her silhouette through the misty glass door. Mindless of the possibility for getting wet, Van opened the door and stuck her head in for a kiss.

"I've got everything ready to start dinner, just say when."

Lauren gave a tired smile. "As much as I'd like to stay in here for an hour, I don't think the hot water will last so I'll be out in ten."

Lauren found Van in the kitchen watching a pot of water on the stove. She moved behind her and slid her arms around Van's waist.

"A watched pot, you know."

Van turned in the circle of Lauren's arms and pulled her close. "Mmm, you smell delicious. I missed you today."

"You say that every day." Lauren rested her cheek against Van's chest.

"That's because I miss you every day." Lauren nuzzled closer. "Dinner shortly. You want to pour us a glass of wine?"

Following dinner they sipped the last of their wine. "Whatcha going to do for the next two days?" Van asked as she stood to clear the table.

"I'd like to sleep the days away, but I've got too much to do around here." Plate in hand Lauren joined her at the sink.

"I think you should sleep as much as you want to. You look completely worn out." Van cupped her cheek, lightly stroking her thumb over Lauren's velvety skin.

"That's so thoughtful. If only the house cleaned itself."

Van took Lauren's hand and led her to the living room. Sitting on the opposite end of the couch, she pulled Lauren's feet into her lap and began massaging one socked foot. "I got called up today," Van said.

"Oh," Lauren responded, and then, "oh!" She was sure her face showed the fear she felt. "So…setting up COVID testing or vaccination sites?"

Van swallowed hard. "Neither." Lauren's brows rose. "Security in DC." Lauren frowned deeply. "Considering what happened at the nation's capitol last week, our government has gotten a clue and doesn't want to take any chances at the Inauguration. They've canceled all the requests from groups to gather, but government is concerned there's still potential for trouble."

Lauren sighed. "And you'll be smack in the middle of it if there is."

"Honey, it's what I do when I'm needed. I don't want you to worry though. There will be so many National Guard troops there. I don't believe anything will get out of control. They're just being overly cautious."

"Uh-huh."

"I promise I'll be safe."

Later when Lauren moved into Van's arms in their bed, Van sensed Lauren's unease. She kissed the top of her head.

"When do you have to leave?" Lauren's breath was warm across Van's chest.

"In the morning."

Lauren looked up into Van's unreadable dark eyes. "For how long?"

Van stroked her fingers through Lauren's long curls. "It's a few days before inauguration and I wouldn't think more than the day or two after. Four maybe five days tops. I hope…"

Lauren kissed her skin and moved up to capture Van's lips. "You're not leaving until I've loved every inch of you." She positioned herself on top of Van's body.

Van kissed Lauren awake at six thirty in the morning. Lauren moaned, reminding Van of their love making last night. "I'm sorry to wake you up so early, but I've got to get a move on."

She covered Lauren's lips with a kiss that spoke of the passion that still burned hot in their marriage after fifteen years together. Two Afghanistan tours for Van during her ten-year enlistment, and most recently Lauren's ten months of hell working in the COVID unit at Athens Regional Hospital in southeastern Ohio.

"I love you more than life," Van said.

Lauren slipped her fingers through Van's short hair. "Sweetheart, I love you every bit as much." She pulled Van down for another passion-filled kiss.

Van finally had to pull away. "I'll call you every evening."

Lauren tried for a genuine smile, but wasn't sure she pulled it off.

"Relax and enjoy your days off. I'll call you this evening." And then Van was gone.

Lauren snuggled back down into the covers and drifted off. Surprisingly she didn't wake up until almost noon. When she dragged herself out of the bed she felt like she'd barely slept. Coffee didn't even sound good so she put water on for tea while she went to find the thermometer. Her temperature was only one hundred degrees. Nothing to worry about. Maybe all the exhausting months of over-work had caught up. Hours later she got a small burst of energy and cleaned the bathroom. Afterward she settled on the couch with her dinner of chicken noodle soup and buttered toast to watch the evening news. She hoped for a glimpse of Van, but more than anything wanted to hear there was peace in our nation's capitol. The broadcaster's words and images of hundreds of military troops on the empty streets reassured her. She woke at one o'clock in the morning curled up on the couch, the TV still on, her half-eaten dinner on the coffee table and with no desire to do anything more than go crawl into bed. So she did.

A loud banging stirred her. At first, she thought it was in her head. It felt awful. She soon realized someone was pounding at the front door. She pulled on her robe while shuffling to answer it. Her body felt as though she'd run a marathon. A quick peek revealed their neighbor, Christine, from across the street and two doors down. She grabbed a mask from the entry table and opened the door.

"Are you okay?" Christine asked her forehead wrinkled with concern.

Lauren smothered a yawn under her mask. "Just tired. All the hours I've been working are killing me. You want to come in?"

Christine shook her head. "Vanessa called me because she hasn't been able to reach you. She said she started trying yesterday evening."

"Oh." Lauren tilted her head.

"Are you sure you're okay?"

"Yeah, I'm fine. The sound is probably off on my phone and buried in my purse wherever I left it last."

"Okay." Lauren could see Christine's smile in her eyes. "Well, let her know everything is okay. She sounded worried to death."

"I'm on it, and thanks."

Christine gave a nod. "That's what neighbors are for."

Gathering her robe up around her neck she located her phone, where she left it in her purse sitting on the dryer and immediately texted Van.

Sweetheart, I'm so sorry to worry you. I left my phone sound off in my purse in the laundry room. I'm super tired and just forgot. I looked for you on the evening news last night. Call me later. I'll be waiting.

She lazed on the couch drinking tea all afternoon. The phone startled her awake in the darkness. She fumbled it from her robe pocket. "Hi." She tried not to sound as groggy as she felt.

"I miss you so much. It's no fun sleeping on the cold marble with mostly guys. It reminds me of Afghanistan, only freezing cold instead of blistering hot."

Lauren rubbed at her temple, a headache making its way across her forehead. ell, like you said it's only for a few days. I miss you too, sweetheart."

"Are you relaxing?"

"Oh yeah, I can't tell you how many hours I've slept these last two days."

"Are you sure everything is all right?"

"Mmm," Lauren murmured. "I needed these days to rest my body."

Van talked for another ten minutes about what she was seeing and experiencing in DC. "As much as I'd like to keep you on here for hours, I need to get back and you need to finish resting up before you have to go back to work in the morning."

"I love you." Lauren made a kissing sound.

"I love you right back, honey. I'll talk to you again tomorrow after your shift is up."

Lauren's phone rang to voice mail again. Van had already left four other messages starting around seven-forty when she knew Lauren should have been home from work. It wasn't quite ten o'clock so she dialed Christine's number.

"I would have to assume she's not home since her car isn't over there. Unless...it's under an invisibility cloak." Christine giggled.

Van tried at a chuckle. "Okay, thanks Christine. I'll track her down."

Now Van was worried to death. Was Lauren still working? Van knew Lauren left her phone in her locker when she was on the clock, but wouldn't Lauren have at least messaged Van to let her know she was working late? She repeatedly rubbed her hand across her hair. She paced, antsy and hyperaware of the smallest sounds inside the massive hall. Waiting another fifteen minutes she dialed Lauren again. This time she heard the distinctive click.

"Lauren Harris's phone."

Van's heart stopped before dropping to her stomach. She couldn't get a breath.

"Hello," the voice sounded in her ear.

Van cleared her throat. "I...I'm trying to reach Lauren. Who is this?"

"Lydia, I'm a nurse at Athens Regional. And you are?"

Van gasped for a breath. She coughed to clear the constriction in her throat, managing to say, "I'm her wife," barely loud enough to be heard. There was a whoosh and the background noises that hadn't registered before were gone. It was dead silent. "Oh, god," she whispered.

"Van," the woman said. "I've been working with Lauren for months, and now I'm her nurse. She has COVID, but there's every reason to think she will be just fine."

Van released the breath she was holding. "Can I talk to her?"

"She's resting really well right now and has a lot of drugs in her. How about if I tell her when she does wake up that you called and have her give you a call then?"

"Uh...okay, I guess, if all I can do is wait." Her voice cracked and tears pricked in her eyes. "Please...please, call me even if she can't talk."

"Of course, sweetie, we will."

"T…thank you for taking care of her."

"She's going to be all right. Believe that, okay?"

"Okay."

"Listen," Lydia continued, "you should arrange a COVID test for yourself, assuming you've been together over the last week."

"Will do." Van was barely keeping it together. She ended the call and wept silently into her sleeve.

"Hey, you okay?" Rich asked. His gentle touch on her shoulder a little bit of comfort.

Van gathered herself and lifted her head. "My wife's in the hospital with COVID."

"Ah damn. Man that sucks."

Van nodded. She and Rich had served together during her last deployment to the Middle East. Rich was a good guy. He never gave Van a hard time because she was a woman in "a man's army," and he was totally cool with her marital status.

"So are you going to skip out? I would if it was my wife in the hospital with that nasty stuff."

"You think he'll let me go? I heard we're supposed to be here until early next week."

"Give me a minute or two then we'll go ask him." He disappeared into the mass of soldiers and when he returned he slid an arm across her shoulder. "Let's go see if we can get you a pass from Cap."

Once they located him Van pleaded her case. "Sir, I've just learned that my spouse has been hospitalized with COVID. I need to get a COVID test and I'd like to request relief of my assignment to return home." She battled back the tears reforming in her eyes.

Rich, standing beside her said, "I've arranged with Juan to cover her shift, Sir. She will be missed on her assignment, but we've got her covered."

Their captain nodded. "You realize, Herrera, that the military cannot transport you."

"Yes, Sir."

"All right. Be sure Sergeant Miller is notified so she can adjust the schedule. She can get the test arranged for you as well. Go be with your loved one, Herrera."

"Yes, Sir. Thank you, Sir."

She saluted and reported to Sgt. Miller, got her test then headed to a quiet spot to figure out her transportation to get home. She found a D.C. to Columbus flight via Atlanta and bought a bus ticket that would get her from the airport in Columbus to Athens. If she were lucky she'd be able to comfort Lauren from home before noontime tomorrow. Her phone pinged with a message stating her COVID test was negative. Lauren had COVID and she'd been with her less than forty-eight hours ago. Van didn't trust the accuracy of those instant tests. She'd contact her own doctor when she got home and get another test to be safe.

Her phone rang with Lauren's number as she whiled away the hours waiting for the plane that would carry her back to Ohio. It would be a long seven and a half hours.

"Hey, honey," Van answered quietly.

Someone cleared their throat. "Uh, sorry, Vanessa?"

"Yes," Van replied.

"This is Janet from Athens Regional. I had strict instructions to call you when Lauren was awake enough to talk to you. Here she is."

A rattling cough preceded a barely audible, "Van."

"I'm here honey. I'm actually at the airport. Coming home and I should be there by lunch tomorrow." Lauren coughed again. "Are they taking good care of you?" Van's heart raced like a thoroughbred, when Lauren coughed again. The sound made her shiver.

"I feel so awful, Van. I want to die."

Van blinked back tears. "No, honey, you don't. Remember wedding vows and all that?" Tears fell down Van's cheeks. "Besides, we haven't had our babies yet." She could hear Lauren struggling to get a breath.

"I'm so tired." She barely heard Lauren say.

"You just need a lot of rest, to follow doctor's orders and I'll be right outside before you know it. I love you, Lauren."

"You too," Lauren whispered.

"Can you give your phone back to Janet, honey?"

"Yes," the stranger's voice sounded in Van's ear.

"She sounds really bad. Are you sure she's going to be okay?"

"We're treating aggressively with a cocktail of medications and I think she'll recover without the need of a ventilator."

"Oh, god," Van muttered.

"She's a real fighter and she's got tons of support here. I know telling you to try and not worry will go in one ear and out the other. At least for Lauren's sake take care of your own health so you can care for her when she comes home."

"I'll try. So when will I be able to talk to her again?"

"I'd say maybe midmorning tomorrow. Don't be alarmed if the phone isn't answered. There isn't someone in here every minute. Just keep trying until you catch one of us."

"Got it, and Janet, thanks for taking care of my wife."

"You're very welcome."

Van disconnected, keeping a death grip on her phone, like a lifeline to Lauren. She thought the waiting was grueling to simply get out of DC, but there was a plane change and hours' long layover in Atlanta before heading on to Columbus. The night seemed endless.

A bit of relief settled over her when she finally boarded the Greyhound for home. But, the relief was short-lived as the road rolled past and she had nothing to think about except the love of her life lying in a hospital bed battling a virus that was killing hundreds of thousands of people. An Uber took her from the bus station to the armory to get her truck and she finally pulled into their drive a few minutes after eleven. She dialed Lauren's phone the second after she dropped her duffel inside the door and herself in her recliner.

Finally, just after noon she reached Lydia.

"She's really out of it on the meds. I don't think she's coherent enough to converse."

"Can we try? I'd like to at least hear the sound of her voice." But, all Van could hear was a moan.

"I'm sorry, she seems to be a little more alert later in the day. I'll leave a message for next shift to call you if she's not awake before I leave, like yesterday. Okay?"

"Sure." Van felt anything but sure as she hung up.

She tried watching a basketball game on TV, but her mind constantly drifted to Lauren and how beautiful she'd looked lying in bed the morning Van had left. The ringing phone startled her awake.

"Hello."

"Vanessa, this is Misty calling for our gal, Lauren Harris."

"How is she?"

"Well, she sleeps like Snow White, but she's kind of awake at the moment and I'm going to hold the phone for you to talk to her."

Van waited a long heartbeat. "Hi honey, it's me bugging you to make sure you're following orders."

All Van heard was "Mmm."

"I know you're super tired and feel terrible, but they are going to fix you up." She didn't delay the call any longer.

Van dropped her phone on the end table and scrubbed her hands over her face. She slumped back in the chair. Her stomach growled reminding her she'd not eaten a thing since early morning. She was beat, but she got up and went to shower. Standing under the spray of hot water the worst imaginable thought occurred to her. What would she do if this virus took Lauren from her? She slid down in the corner on the cold tile and sobbed. She'd never be able to sleep in their bed without Lauren beside her. Not tonight or any night. She grabbed a bottle of water, a throw and got comfortable in the recliner. Maybe she would sleep...maybe.

The ringing phone woke Van around seven thirty in the morning.

"Hello?" Van covered a yawn.

"Van, this is Lydia from the hospital."

The woman's voice sounded too official. *No, no, no.* Van's head spun and bile rose to the back of her throat.

"Hello…Van," Lydia said.

Van managed a "yes," the phone shaking in her hand.

"So, Lauren's fever broke at about one o'clock this morning. She's doing better by the minute. If her recovery stays on this course, she'll probably be released in a day or two."

Van exhaled audibly. "Is she awake now?"

"She is, hold on."

"Sweetheart." As scratchy as Lauren's voice sounded there wasn't a sweeter sound to Van's ears.

"I'm so happy to hear your voice I don't know what to say."

Lauren coughed and cleared her throat. "That would be a first, I think."

Van chuckled. "Lydia tells me you're on your way to escaping that place."

Lauren coughed and cleared her throat again. "Yeah. Being a patient here is definitely less fun than working here and you know how draining that's been."

"I know, honey. I'm just so happy you're on the mend."

"Not more than me. I love you more than life, and no offense intended, but I'm so happy that it doesn't feel like you're sitting on my chest now."

Van laughed. It felt so good to have a reason to feel light-hearted. "No offense taken, honey. This little crisis hit so close to home."

"It did." Lauren drew an audible breath and exhaled it.

"I should let you go so you can rest and come home all the sooner."

"Call me later."

"You can count on it. I love you, Lauren."

"I love you, Van Herrera." She made a kissing sound and they ended their call.

PRIVATE SHOW

Riley Scott

The gentle hum of her calming playlist drew to a close, just as Christina Villanova hit send on her last email of the day. Closing her laptop screen, she stretched her neck side to side and stood. The ceiling fan whirred overhead, and outside her window, she could hear the song of a bird perched in one of the trees. With a glance at the growing to-do list on the white board she'd hung above her desk, she sighed and closed her eyes. Bringing her fingers to massage her temples and willing the stress of the day to fade into oblivion, she took a deep breath.

"You've done enough for the day," she whispered the mantra she'd adopted since her days had somehow grown even busier in a time when the world seemed to be at a standstill.

Her head pounded, and she wished she could have eased the ache with a soothing cup of coffee, instead of another decaf tea. Glancing down at the sad, tepid liquid in the mug on her desk, she grimaced. She blinked, trying to clear her eyes from the lingering effects of one too many Zoom calls. Why everyone suddenly needed to see people every second of the day, she would never understand.

As she made her way to the living room of the quaint villa, she looked around the room for Raven. Her frown lifted into a smile as she looked out the window, where Raven was crouched, pruning the vegetable plants in the garden she'd started cultivating during her extra time at home. Putting her hands on her hips, Chris watched the grace and care with which she maneuvered the shears—the same precision with which those skilled hands did everything, from tuning a guitar to delighting every inch of Chris's body.

Chris looked around the room with pride. Around her, the walls were adorned with art from their travels, framed photographs, and homey touches, something that felt like such a far cry from the crowded tour bus where their journey had begun. Biting her lip, she eyed Raven. Her once wild and untamed rockstar of a wife now devoted her quarantine days to growing beets and jalapeños, working in the yard, and doting on Chris.

"We're pretty lucky," Chris whispered so as not to disturb Raven's handiwork in the garden. She placed a protective hand over her swelling stomach, smiling down at the growing life inside of her. "Your mommy is a badass."

Checking the clock on the wall, she decided she'd give Raven another half hour before reminding her to clean up for the home concert she was throwing this evening. Not that she could have forgotten, Chris reminded herself. While the pandemic had uprooted their lives as much as it had the rest of the world, Raven still lived and breathed for her fans. Chris's smile grew as she recalled the way Raven lit up any time she was able to play in front of an audience, even virtually.

She headed toward the kitchen, mentally running through a list of dinner options. Stopping in the entryway, she admired the intricately designed tiles of their backsplash, depicting Native American symbols and southwestern designs, for the hundredth time. She stepped back and looked around. She was still as in love with every single detail as she'd been on the day when Raven had surprised her with the villa-style house in Santa Fe— the location of what they always referred to as their first date.

Swept away with nostalgia, Chris walked over, running her fingers along the deep brown tiled countertops. Tears formed in the corners of her eyes. Lucky was an understatement. Clearing her throat, she washed and dried her hands. It would do her no good to give in to the onslaught of hormones she'd been experiencing.

These days, it felt like she went from one end of the spectrum to the other in a flash, with seemingly little to set her off. Today apparently, it was tiles. She washed her hands and set to work, opting for tacos. Quick, easy, and Raven's favorite, the meal would serve as a nice kickoff to their evening.

"Babe!" She heard the front door swing open, Raven's excited voice ringing behind it. Bounding into the kitchen, Raven was covered in dirt, and her fitted cream-colored tee was now ripped. Sweat beaded on her forehead, and her hands were covered in either dried blood or beet juice, Chris couldn't tell which. Chris stifled a laugh and cocked her head to the side in question. "What's up?"

"There's a roadrunner in our yard," she said, her smile lighting up as she threw her hands in the air.

"They are the state bird, you know?" Chris said, laughing and leaning over for a quick kiss, careful not to get covered in the soil that still clung to Raven's clothing and hands.

"Yeah," Raven said and then shook her head. "But this one was in our yard. That's how peaceful it is out there. Come look." She waved Chris over, and despite the ground sirloin sizzling in the pan beside her, Chris couldn't turn down Raven when she looked so full of life.

Raven grabbed Chris's hand, pulling her toward the door. Once on the front porch, Chris breathed in the fresh air, smiling at the result of Raven's hard work. Not only was it as peaceful as she'd said, but it was transformed from the ordinary yard it had been just a few weeks earlier. The neat and tidy raised beds of vegetables were surrounded by Edison party lights strung overhead. The look was made complete with an adorable yard gnome, keeping watch over her plants.

"The roadrunner isn't the best part," Raven said, holding up her hand for Chris to stop. "I'll be right back." She turned and disappeared behind the side of the house, and Chris resisted the urge to follow. Busying herself, she looked through each of the ornately designed and intricately placed raised beds. Everything was crafted so purposefully. She bit her lip, marveling at the mystery that was Raven. Somehow she could be so free and wild, yet so precise and careful.

"This is for you," Raven said, heaving a large Adirondack chair into the clearing beside her garden. "The paint just dried." She smiled down at the chair and back up at Chris, wiping her brow.

"Did you…" Chris trailed off, tears returning to the corners of her eyes once more. "Did you make this?"

Raven shoved her hands in her pockets and stood straighter. She nodded, while her tightlipped smile highlighted her dimple. Closing the distance between them and no longer caring about the dirt, Chris wrapped her arms around Raven's neck, pulling her close. Her smile was still on her lips as she kissed Raven. "I love you so damn much."

Leaning back, Raven laughed. "I love you too," she said, kissing Chris's forehead. "Maybe I should build you things more often," she added with a wink.

"Yeah? Maybe you should. You are pretty good with those hands."

Raven bit her lip and nodded, her mouth twisting into a grin. "I'll show you what I can do with these hands."

Chris took a seat in her chair and smiled up at Raven, as she straddled Chris and lowered herself carefully to hover right above the spot where Chris craved her touch. Raven tangled her hands in Chris's hair, soliciting a moan as she kissed her way down her neck. Chris arched her back, desire muddling her thoughts.

"Soon baby," Raven said, kissing her collarbone gently, before standing up and offering a hand up. "Right now I have to get cleaned up." She glanced down at the simple wood and leather watch on her wrist, shaking it to remove some of the dirt with a laugh. "I need to hop in the shower and do hair and makeup."

Chris cleared her throat and looked down at her own shirt, now streaked with dirt. "I should change and finish the tacos." Her eyes widened. "Tacos! Shit! Go shower," she said, ushering Raven inside, and hustling over to the stove, thankful to find that the meat was only slightly crisp. Removing the pan from the stove, she pulled out a bite and let it cool before sampling. It would have to do. Glancing at the clock, she nodded. It was go time. There was no time to change. As if she was on a timed cooking show, she worked as quickly as she could manage. She fried up the tortillas, chopped the veggies, and was putting the finishing touches on her homemade guacamole by the time Raven rounded the corner, practically dripping in sex appeal.

Dressed in a tight black tank, paired with ripped jeans and chucks, she could have very easily been headed to the store, but her winged eyeliner, smoky eye and sultry dark lipstick told a different story. "Is this okay?" she asked, looking at Chris with one eyebrow raised.

"Yeah," Chris said, drying her hands on the towel by the stove. "Sorry, I got a bit distracted." She walked over and looped her fingers through Raven's belt loops, pulling her closer until she could feel her hips grind against her body. "You look like the type of rockstar whose tour bus I'd sneak onto just for a minute or two of privacy." She trailed her fingers down, over the outline of Raven's full breasts, clenching her teeth as she felt a shiver of anticipation course through her veins.

"If memory serves me correctly, you and a tour bus once created quite the deliciously dirty combination." Raven's body swayed against her, and Chris tensed. She wished they had more time. Settling for a kiss, she took Raven's bottom lip gently in her own, before biting it lightly.

"I want you." Chris sighed as she deepened the kiss.

"I find it amazing that you're not sick of me yet." Raven's husky laugh rang through the kitchen. "We've been cooped up together for months, and somehow it still feels like we're in this magical stage of our relationship."

"First of all," Chris said, placing a kiss on Raven's forehead, "I could never be sick of you. Second of all, I know what you mean. We're so lucky. I had to listen to Linda yammer on this afternoon about how much she can't stand to be around Jimmy during all of this, and I just couldn't relate." She thought to how many of the work acquaintances she'd heard complain about being quarantined with their spouses, and counted herself lucky to not be among them. "Somehow this whole experience has allowed me to get to know you even more, and it's made me love you that much more." She leaned her head on Raven's shoulder. "I can't thank you enough for this year. You've held me together and built me up, while somehow also letting me fall apart from time to time." Leaning back to look in Raven's eyes, she smirked. "And you've done it all while looking sexy as hell."

"Me?" Raven laughed, running her fingers through her messy hair. "Have you looked in a mirror lately?" She shook her head, looking Chris up and down with a sideways grin.

Chris laughed, placing her hands on her belly with a nod. "I've seen myself, yes. All of myself."

Raven shook her head and placed a finger under Chris's chin, tilting her head up for another kiss. "You are a vision and one hot baby mama."

"I'm glad you think so." Chris basked in the embrace for a second longer, before clearing her throat. "I made tacos," she said, gesturing to the array of food and toppings neatly displayed behind her on the chile-shaped silver tray Raven had gifted her for Valentine's Day. "You should eat while you have a few minutes."

"Mmm," Raven growled. "Hot baby mama, a concert and tacos. I'm not sure what I did to deserve all this."

"Feeling's mutual, babe." She watched Raven make her plate, piling the tacos high with lettuce, tomatoes, green chile, cheese, and sour cream. Living in the Land of Enchantment sure had opened up their eyes to a handful of new, spicy traditions. Her eyes trailed lower, watching Raven's hips sway to a beat only she could hear. Shoving her hands in her pockets, Chris made a mental note of all the places she'd like to grab later.

Resting up against the counter, she followed suit and made her plate, before taking her place across from Raven at the table.

"How was work?" Raven asked before taking a giant bite of her meal.

Chris glanced down at her tacos and shook her head. "Nothing new to report. Same as every day since March, I guess." She shrugged, taking a bite so she didn't have to elaborate. Even though she knew she should just feel gratitude—and most of the time she did—the fog of depression and uncertainty still hung over every moment.

"Yoga and a back rub after the concert," Raven offered, smiling sweetly at Chris and leveling her gaze. "You and our baby need to stay rested up."

"Deal," Chris agreed. "Have you watched any of the news today?"

Raven cleared her throat and wiped the corners of her lips with a napkin. "I caught bits and pieces this morning before I went to work in the garden. I know we've got it a lot better than most." She glanced over her shoulder into the kitchen. "I'm going to go through our pantry and do another drop-off, along with a check, to the food bank this weekend."

"I love your heart," Chris said, looking down at the plate in front of her, then back to Raven. "You really are as good as gold."

"Nah," Raven said, waving a hand through the air. "It's not just the news." She sighed, her shoulders falling. "I've been hearing so many stories from everyone on social media, and I know people are really struggling."

"You're doing so much. The concert, the donations, and not to mention reaching out to so many of your fans." Chris reached her hand across the table, wrapping her fingers through Raven's. The weight of Raven's empathy hung between them. As someone who had always thrived when in the company of others, she'd watched Raven go through the various stages of depression, only to be refueled by a mission to rejuvenate, inspire and help others, all while writing a slew of brand-new songs she'd yet to debut.

Raven glanced at her guitar in the living room and sighed. "It's not much," she said, shaking her head. "But maybe it'll offer a spark of hope for some."

"Everyone has been in their homes for months. I'm sure they'll be over the moon to hear you perform."

Raven nodded. She glanced at her watch and pushed her plate aside. "I'll do the dishes later," she said, dabbing her napkin on her lips. "Did I mess up my makeup?"

"No," Chris said, smiling as she stood. "But I will later."

To her relief, Raven smiled and pulled her in for a hug. "I'll hold you to that. For now, I've got to go make some music."

"Make the magic happen, babe," Chris said, giving her a playful pat on the ass.

Raven turned on her heel and eyed Chris with a new spark in her eye. "I know it's not technically a show with all the glitz and glamor we used to have," she said, grabbing Chris's waist and pulling her closer, "but what do you say we keep up tradition?"

Raising an eyebrow, Chris nodded. "It's my favorite tradition," she said, wrapping her arms around Raven's neck and kissing her with a hunger for more.

"Mine too," Raven said, pulling back from the embrace after a moment. "And, I think it's just what we needed for a good show."

As Raven made her way to the couch, Chris ran her fingers across her bottom lip, where the taste of Raven still lingered. Smiling, she thought back to every time they'd kissed for good luck before one of Raven's shows. Behind the curtain, the crowds would roar and the lights would flash, but all of it would fade when Raven took her into her arms and pressed her body up against Chris's, and for a moment, the world would stand still. She'd basked in that moment, knowing that somehow, out of all the women in the world, she'd been the one made to be Raven's other half. Then, she'd get to enjoy the show from her special backstage seat, marveling as the love of her life displayed her epic talents for thousands of adoring fans.

She took a deep breath. Just as she'd promised Raven, those days would return at some point. For now, this would suffice.

Settling into her favorite recliner, just off screen, she leaned back, admiring how Raven kicked off the live stream with every ounce of energy she would have displayed in person.

"I know it's a scary time," Raven said, looking into the camera, "and my heart goes out to each and every one of you—from the frontline workers, to those who are sick or have lost loved ones, everyone whose mental health is suffering, and all who are struggling financially. I want you to know that I'm here for you. I know many of you have reached out via direct messages, and I'm doing my best to respond to all of those. I also want you to know that, even in a time like this, music can heal the soul. So without further ado, let's dive right in."

As she strummed her guitar and the first riff hit the air, Chris felt a kick in her stomach. Stifling a laugh, she placed a hand over her belly, making a mental note to let Raven know that their little rockstar enjoyed the performance. Closing her eyes, Chris let Raven's sultry voice calm every worry in her body.

As she wrapped up the final song on her set list, Chris couldn't help but imagine the screams and cheers of fans, mixed in with their sea of voices singing Raven's words back to her. She shook her head, smiling in awe at Raven. Even after all the years, she'd never get over the power of her talent. Quietly, she stood, making her way to the kitchen for a drink, as Raven started a question-and-answer session in the chat.

Chris leaned against the wall and listened as Raven spoke to everything from her makeup routine to her garden, the tacos she'd eaten for dinner, an update on Chris and the baby, and new music in the works. She had to admire the openness with which Raven approached her fame. It definitely made her job as Raven's head publicist a little easier than it had once been.

From the living room, Raven bid farewell to the fans tuning in to the live stream and exited out of the screen, before closing her laptop. She propped her guitar up on the couch next to her and let out a sigh.

She leaned back into the couch. "That was amazing," she said, shaking her head. "It's just not quite the same. You know?"

"I know." Chris filled her glass of water and smiled mischievously to herself as an idea formed. "What do you miss most?" she asked, buying some time, while Raven flipped through the social media channels on her phone, no doubt answering questions from fans who still lingered in the comment sections.

"I miss it all," she said, not looking up. "I miss the thrill of the crowd, the lights, the rush that fills my soul when the first beat comes through those speakers and rattles my bones. I miss the fans."

Reaching behind her back, Chris unclasped her bra. She grinned, not wanting to ruin the sincerity of Raven's moment, but also wanting to pull her from the darkness for a moment of gratitude and humor. "You miss your groupies, babe?" She kept her tone upbeat and amused.

"What?" Raven asked. She jerked her head up, just in time to catch Chris's black lace bra in her face. Standing in the doorway, Chris winked as Raven ran her fingers over the material.

Raven bit her lip and placed her phone on the coffee table, never breaking eye contact. "I asked, if you missed your groupies," Chris said, lowering her voice, as she closed the distance between them. Raven moved to stand, but Chris shook her head, placing her hands firmly on Raven's shoulders. "If it's the rush and the adoration of your fans you're missing, why don't you give me a backstage tour and maybe play a little private show for an audience of one?"

With a low moan, Raven looped her fingers through the hem of Chris's shirt and pulled it over her head in one smooth motion.

"God, that still turns me on every bit as much as it did the first time," Chris said, breathless as Raven wrapped her thick lips around one of Chris's nipples. In response, Raven moved her kiss lower, but Chris pulled back, shaking her head.

"What's wrong?" Raven's voice had diminished to a whimper, desperate with need.

"I'm pretty sure you're the one who's supposed to be getting the rockstar treatment," Chris said, biting her lip. Sliding down to her knees, she unbuttoned Raven's pants. Arching her back,

Raven let Chris slide them down and toss them to the side. "And I'm the one showing my utter gratitude for such an incredible performance," she added, leaning in to place a tender kiss on Raven's inner thigh.

Raven gasped and leaned her head back. As Chris's tongue played against the soft material of Raven's boyshorts, she thrust her hips forward, intensifying the pressure.

Pulling the thin material out of the way, Chris savored Raven's labored breaths. She looked up, watching as desire danced in Raven's eyes.

"Please, baby," she moaned.

Unable to resist such an urgent plea, Chris tasted Raven's wetness. Swirling her tongue in rhythm, she matched Raven's panting breaths, delighting in the feeling of Raven's hands tangling in her hair.

Lost in the taste of her wife and the soft moans filling the air, Chris closed her eyes and felt her gratitude swell. Even if their world looked nothing like it had months earlier, she plunged her tongue deeper, knowing there was nowhere else she'd rather be.

The characters in this short story first appeared in the novel Backstage Pass *by Riley Scott.* Backstage Pass *is available from Bella Books or your favorite retailer.*

LOST

Laina Villeneuve

"I need your help," Kristine said once she and Robyn reached the wide part of the trail in the redwoods where they could ride side by side. Kristine still rode her paint mule Bean, and Robyn rode a sorrel mare she had bought years before.

"Everything okay?" Robyn asked.

Kristine blew out a long breath. Robyn Landy, bowl-maker, gardener, and the best kind of friend was always available to listen without judgment and never offered platitudes. "Gloria's on the hairy edge."

"Oh. What's going on?"

"She needs a break."

"Don't we all?"

"Yes, but she doesn't take them. I feel guilty every time I come to the barn, but she insists that I need to get away to stay sane."

"You do," Robyn agreed.

"I know I do, and I've said she needs to stop, but she can't ever get away from her worries. She's taking the "Safer at

Home" order really hard and is completely stressed out. There are literally no breaks with everyone on top of each other. But if I say I'll take the kids to the park to get them out of her hair, she's worried about whether it's safe. That's not a break."

"Please don't tell me you want me to watch your kids," Robyn's voice squeaked. "Don't you remember that time I lost Caemon?"

"Robyn, that was six years ago! I'm not asking you to watch the kids. It's Bean. Can you watch him for a week? I know it's a lot to ask, but I need to get Gloria out of here. Caemon told me the last time they were over at his granddad's house, he found his mom in the old camper. It got me thinking…" Though it was going on ten years since she had met Gloria in the High Sierras, remembering the surprise of finding Gloria's camper moved just down the road from the pack station where she worked still made her smile. It had been too long since they had escaped. They had been promising themselves they would take their two kids back to The Lodge when they were both big enough to ride, and then COVID hit.

"Thinking about the backcountry?"

"Yeah. All of us are on the Internet so much…I think it would be good to go to the mountains. Get Gloria away from the news…We need to let the house air out."

At this, Robyn laughed. "I know exactly what you mean. The air starts to push on you, doesn't it? I'm lucky I can still turn my bowls in my shop and come out here to take care of Caramel. Grace is glued to her computer, just like Gloria. Even after dinner, she's still standing there answering emails like she can fix the world if she gets to every single one in her inbox."

"Would it be too much to ask you to take care of Bean?"

A wicked smile played on Robyn's lips. "It actually might be tough for me to swing. Maybe call Grace and see if she can help you out."

Kristine caught on quickly. "Since she's working from home, I doubt she'd be coming out in her designer clothes like she did when Eliza was born."

"She might if you told her how fun it would be for me to watch her try to keep Bean's slobber off her jacket."

Kristine studied her friend. Robyn and Grace shared a big house, and since Robyn was retired from the Coast Guard, only Grace was working remotely. They had no kids, so she figured they must have been taking advantage of the extra time together.

"What is going on in that head of yours? You just turned so red!"

"These last months, by the time we get to the end of the day, Gloria and I are just…spent. I guess, well I thought…"

Robyn slapped her thigh and filled the forest with her laugh. "You thought we were having sex every day?"

"Something like that."

"Sorry to disappoint you. Stress is not the best aphrodisiac. I have no excuse to be so exhausted, but I am wiped out every single day. Mentally as much as physically." They rode in silence for a few minutes, and then Robyn said, "Ask Grace to take care of Bean. It will be good for her to get away from the computer and remember how hot she thinks I am in my riding breeches. That might put her in the mood for a roll in the hay."

Robyn got a faraway look on her face and then turned to Kristine. "Have you ever had a literal roll in the hay? I always worried it would be super itchy. But maybe a literal roll in the hay would be fun!"

Kristine plugged her ears with her fingers. "La, la, la, la, la."

If it had been only Kristine and Gloria heading out on a road trip, they could have made the drive from the coastal town of Eureka to The Lodge in the High Sierras in one day. Kristine knew better than to try to pull a ten-hour trip with two young children. She phoned her brother.

"Hypothetically, what's the likelihood we could see you if we happened to be in Quincy?"

"Why would you be in Quincy?" Gabe asked.

"It's halfway to The Lodge." There was a long silence. "I know we can't stay with you and we can't hug you, but it would be so good to see you."

"You're going to The Lodge?"

His wistfulness made Kristine want to extend an invitation to him, but she knew he was in no position to go. "I'm sorry I can't ask you along."

"Me too. Brenna's been worried about the hospitals being overcrowded and seems to think that since I've seen a mare drop a foal, I can somehow help her get the baby out when it's time."

Kristine chortled. "No pressure!" Gabe chuckled nervously, making Kristine's heart ache. How would she be able to resist throwing her arms around her solid brother if they got to see him?

"Are you really coming through?"

"We've got to get away. Being holed up here isn't doing any of us any good. I have a plan."

"I'm all ears," Gabe said.

* * *

Gloria was tired. She didn't remember the last time she had felt rested and didn't see how a road trip was supposed to recharge her batteries. Every stop on this trip would make her worry about how they were increasing their exposure to the virus. Pushing their luck. But getting out made Kristine happy. Thank goodness because someone had to venture to the store. These days all she wanted was to crawl in a cave and sleep until things went back to normal, back to when she could drop the kids off at school and work without distraction.

"Look at the horse, Mama!" Eliza shrieked as Kristine pulled up to Hot Rocks Resort. "Can we ride him?"

"No, we'll ride when we get to The Lodge. We're just going to stay here, so we can see Gramma and Grandpa Owens without worrying about getting them sick."

The extra weight of potentially bringing COVID to Kristine's family threatened to dampen Gloria's mood further, but the huge white horse in front of the car bobbed his head playfully as if to suggest she shake the thoughts from her head.

"Can we pet him?" Eliza asked as she launched herself from the car.

"Masks!" Gloria ordered, scrambling out of the car to hand them to both children before they approached the horse.

"He looks friendly enough," Kristine said, petting his broad face. The kids squealed with delight as the horse nuzzled their ball caps. Kristine met Gloria's eyes and smiled. She was trying so hard to help, Gloria could see that, but everything was muted. She was standing right next to Kristine, yet she felt so far away.

"That's Houdini," a woman said from the porch. She was petite and wore her brown hair shorter than Kristine's. She unrolled the sleeves of a flannel she wore loose over a tee as she approached them. Despite the fact that she wore a face mask, Gloria could tell she had a big smile on her face. "And I'm Madison. Welcome to Hot Rocks!"

"It's so nice to finally meet you!" Kristine said. She had worked with Madison for years, ever since they collaborated to decorate the resort with Kristine's photographs which her guests were welcome to buy. They had only ever communicated online.

"I wasn't sure if you'd be open, but Gabe said you haven't been hit too hard."

"No, I've been really lucky! Friends like Gabe recommend their relatives stay here to escape. The separate cabins make it easy for guests to keep clear of each other, and with Cup of Joy providing all the meals, you don't have to go into town at all."

"Sweet. How's Lacey's shop doing?"

"Hardly anyone needs repairs these days with the 'Stay at Home' order, but so far, she's kept herself busy refurbishing old cars."

"I'm so glad to hear that," Kristine said.

"Come on in, and I'll get you set up with the keys to your cabin."

Kristine rubbed Gloria's shoulders as she passed, another reminder to relax. They were on vacation.

"Mommy, feel how soft Houdini is," Eliza said. Gloria stroked the horse's long neck. While she could appreciate how much Bean helped Kristine recalibrate each day, horses did not lift her spirit. Kristine kept telling her that she needed a hobby, something besides the news. Everything Kristine suggested made her feel so tired. She did not want to start a garden or a puzzle or a scrapbook. There was already too much to be done.

She felt Kristine behind her and leaned into her embrace.

"Hear that?" Kristine asked.

"What?"

"The trees saying welcome home."

"The trees talk to you, Mama?" Eliza asked. Caemon rolled his eyes.

"You have to be very still and put everything else out of your mind to hear it." Kristine squeezed Gloria softly before grabbing bags from the car and leading them to the cabin.

The cabin only had one room. The kids would sleep on the couch. It was little more than a wooden box with a kitchenette, rustic furniture, and a pot-bellied stove. Kristine energetically carried in their bags and loaded the kids with their own backpacks and stuffed-animal friends who had joined them on their adventure. "I don't know if this load will ride," she said, pulling on Caemon's backpack. "I might need to add a little more to the front." She stacked a few more pillows in his arms.

"This is a fine mule you made, Gloria!" Kristine hollered toward the cabin.

"I'm telling Uncle Gabe you think he's an ass," Caemon grumbled.

"Caemon said a bad word!" Eliza said.

"Your Uncle Gabe wouldn't mind being called a donkey," Kristine joked.

Gloria loved their ribbing but felt so far removed from it. The way Kristine caught her eye, Gloria could tell she felt it, too. Gloria had to shake herself out of her funk.

"Speaking of Uncle Gabe, he said since we're in town, we have to feed the stock tonight. Give Mommy a hug."

Gloria looked confused but accepted Eliza's hug and Caemon's high five. He was getting too old to accept hugs as often as he used to.

"Take some time for yourself," Kristine said. She cupped Gloria's chin with her hand. "We'll be safe. We'll keep our masks on the whole time and promise to stay outside and six feet apart. You take care of you. The blue backpack has some things I thought you might like if you don't feel like hiking or napping."

Gloria didn't know what to say. Kristine kissed her with a gentle forcefulness, her lips a reminder of their connection. Gloria could be out of sorts, and Kristine wasn't going anywhere. Except to feed her family's stock.

She watched them pull away and then grabbed the backpack before sitting in the doorway, her legs stretched in front of her. She began lifting out treats, a container of dark chocolate peanut butter cups, some dark chocolate nut clusters Gloria loved to binge on and her favorite vinegar Kettle chips. Underneath, there were three books. Gloria pulled a stickie note from the first one. *It's been a while since you've written me a book report on the lesbian smut you read.*

Gloria opened the chips and read the back of each book. She couldn't believe that Kristine remembered the authors she had read back when they'd met. The "About the Author" section in the crisp new books felt like reuniting with old friends she hadn't seen in too long. How had she missed so many of their new releases? As a nod to her wife, she chose the book with the horse on the cover and opened it to the first page, losing herself immediately.

"You'll ruin your eyes reading in the dark!"

Gloria startled at the voice and then blinked in confusion at just how dark it was. "Hope! It's good to see you." Gloria groaned as she stood. "I'm too old to sit on the floor for hours."

"Hours! Must be a good book!"

"Really good."

Hope surveyed the array of snacks and raised the bags she was holding. "I hope you didn't spoil your dinner. Kristine ordered a lot!"

Gloria stepped outside to allow Hope to put her delivery on their table.

"It's just you?" Hope asked when she rejoined her outside.

"And my book, yes. Kristine took the kids out to the ranch to feed the animals. I had no idea they'd been gone so long. I completely lost myself in the story."

"Who is it?"

Gloria held up the book for her to read the title and author. "Oh, I've read almost everything by her. I loved that baking one of hers so much that I will often pull it off the shelf just to read a chapter."

"You can stop at a chapter?" Gloria asked.

"Most of the time," Hope answered sheepishly. "I keep my favorites in my office, and sometimes I stay later than I should."

"Oh, I miss my office!" When was the last time anyone had reacted to her return home with smiles and hugs? A better question would be when she had last had the house to herself. In a normal, polite, pre-COVID conversation, the next thing to say would have been kid-related, but she did not want to talk about how she had never planned on being a first- and fourth-grade teacher. The novel had her thinking of all sorts of things she would like to do with Kristine that were highly unlikely to happen. She let out a huge breath. "COVID has ruined my sex life."

There was a pause when Gloria wondered whether she had actually voiced her thought, but Hope's surprised laughter answered her question. "Oh my word, isn't that the truth?" she asked.

"I'm sorry! I have no idea why I said that out loud!"

"No, I am right there with you. It took me a long time to get over feeling uncomfortable about Halley living with us, but I finally got to the point where I decided she was one of the ones who encouraged me to follow my heart. She'd want me to feed my libido, right?"

Gloria nodded, encouraging her to continue.

"But then Joy started having nightmares…"

"She's seven now?"

Hope nodded. "But she sounds much bigger when she comes tearing down the hall like a whole herd of horses, banging on the door, and it's always at The. Absolute. Worst. Time. If we're lucky, one of us can get her settled back into bed, but most of the time, it takes her so long to settle back down…"

"The mood is ruined."

"Bingo. It's gotten so bad that we'll just be kissing, not even naked, and I swear I hear something." She shook her head. "And who do you talk to about it?"

"Not your wife!"

"Exactly!"

"And I don't know about you, but I never have a quiet moment to myself at the house to let off some steam." Again, she couldn't believe she had said what she just said, and Hope held her gaze for a few minutes before they both erupted into laughter.

"We thought we were doing pretty well, finding a window in-between when Caemon finally goes to bed and when Eliza comes into our room." Hope gave her an inquisitive look. "Right after the "Safer a Home" order, I started finding Eliza asleep on our floor. She does it so often now that we've built a permanent nest out of couch cushions. She doesn't usually come in until after midnight, so we found a good window…"

"But?"

"One morning, Eliza said at the breakfast table, 'Why is your door sometimes shut, Mommy? I tried the handle last night, and it wouldn't open.'" Gloria hid her red face in her hands. Hope exploded in laughter again and did not have a chance to respond before headlights swept through the pine trees, followed by the sound of slamming doors and kids' voices. "Speak of the devil," Gloria said.

"Hope!" Kristine called in greeting. She instructed the kids to run in and wash their hands for supper. "I just saw Dani and Joy as we were leaving. She was wondering what got you hung up so long."

"I should go. This was just so nice. A little bit of normal to sit and pretend like the world hasn't gone crazy." She looked at Gloria. "Thank you for talking. I hope you get to the good part of the book soon." She waggled her eyebrows and said her goodbyes.

"I didn't mean to scare her off," Kristine said, apologetically.

"You're fine. It's suppertime. Routine, you know?"

Kristine gave her a quick kiss and hug before ushering her inside to check out the dinner Hope had delivered.

Gloria squeezed her extra tightly. "Thank you for the book and the treats. And the time. You were right about needing to get away."

"You feel better?"

Gloria held up the book and then used it to fan herself. "It was really sweet of you to give me that time, but I can't really say I feel better."

"No?" Kristine looked worried.

"Are you kidding me? This has me just about as frustrated as when I was reading her earlier books down at Fish Creek wondering if you liked me at all."

"Good thing we cleared that up," Kristine said, kissing her again until she heard "Ewwww" in stereo from Caemon and Eliza. "Guess we had better feed our beasts."

Before she walked away, Kristine's hand slid down to cup Grace's buttock, sending a shock of sparks through her groin.

* * *

"I may never forgive you," Gloria whispered into Kristine's neck when they finally had the kids asleep.

"What? I thought you said I did good!" Kristine worried for a moment, but Gloria slid her hand under the hem of Kristine's T-shirt and sent a very different message. Her fingertips pulled on Kristine's strings of desire, and she understood. "I miss you."

Gloria pulled Kristine closer, running her hands more possessively along Kristine's curves, pulling her hips and breasts closer. "You did a very good job at getting me hot and bothered. And now what are you going to do about it?"

Kristine found Gloria's skin, pushing her shirt out of the way. "Are you saying you want me to do something about it?"

"In a new place with the kids just now asleep? Forget it. I just wanted you to suffer with me," Gloria hmphed.

"I'm sorry it's so hard."

"I know. And it helps to know that Hope and Dani don't have it much easier."

"What!" Kristine gripped Gloria's back with her nails. "You talked about our sex life?"

"She said COVID's ruined things for them, too. Didn't you talk to Dani while you were out at the ranch?"

"We talked, sure! But we talked about how hard it is to keep students engaged remotely, especially when so much of our classes include hands-on learning."

"That's what you talked about?"

"I did have the kids, you know."

"True." Gloria relaxed into Kristine's arms. "I miss you so much."

Sleep eluded Kristine after Gloria's breathing evened out as she drifted to sleep. Getting away had been a good idea. The change of scenery was good for them all, but she wished that there was a way to ditch the kids and have some time alone with Gloria.

Two days and many winding roads later, Kristine once again descended into the valley leading to The Lodgepole Pine Pack Outfit.

"Look at the sign!" Caemon said after they'd parked by the corral. "The mule's wearing a mask!"

A tall slim figure decked out in chaps and spurs exited the store. "Of course they do. Every mule I've ever met was smarter than most people," she said before taking a big bite of an ice cream bar.

"Don't I know it," Kristine answered. "A good number of the mules in the corral were bred by my family."

The cowgirl started to extend her hand and then shook her head, waving instead. "Great to meet you! I heard you were coming with your family. I'm Jo, and my partner Daisy is going to be leading your ride to Rainbow Falls."

"I want to see the horses!" Eliza yelled.

"Small voices around the horses," Kristine reminded her.

"You take them," Gloria said. "I'll pay up and see when we can check into the cabin.

The kids ran ahead of Kristine and Jo. Though she had her own boots and hat, she felt out of place being guest instead of guide. "Is that Beetle in the dude string?" Her eyes bulged.

"It is," the cowgirl saddling answered. With her black Zorro hat and bandana tied around her face, she looked like a vigilante. "I'm Daisy. You must be the famous Kristine! I'm so excited to finally meet you! Jo says I have to hear you tell the story about how you shot Dozer one summer."

"Mama, you shot someone?" Caemon asked, wide-eyed.

"With a rubber bullet," Kristine said. "And it was an accident."

A loud guffaw rang out behind her as Gloria returned with the receipt in hand. "I look forward to hearing *that* version of the story."

Kristine bowed her head, wishing she could disappear as the adults joined together in shared laughter. "You want a hand getting everyone mounted?" Kristine asked, hoping to redirect everyone's attention.

"Sure! I'd put your little one on Pinkie there. And Bullwinkle would be great for your son," Daisy said.

"Thank you for that," Kristine whispered, grateful for the redirect.

"No, I'm sorry. I don't know what I was thinking saying that in front of your kids."

"That's okay. It's a good story, and it's probably gotten better passed around the campfire over the years. It'd be fun to hear it from you!"

Once they were all aboard their mounts, Daisy greeted everyone and praised them for all wearing masks, "Winning the West for a hundred and fifty years, we say around here! Great for dust, disease, and stagecoach robberies...Let's see if we find any on the wagon trail. Lucky for you, we have our own sharpshooter riding drag today!"

Kristine's cheeks turned red. She was ten years smarter than that version of herself. She'd returned hoping to find direction for her life and had ended up falling in love. Now here she was again, hoping the mountains had some answers for her wife.

When they stopped at Rainbow Falls, Kristine escorted her family down the stairs to the bottom in hopes of catching sight of the rainbow. "See it there?" She pointed. "The sun is just starting to catch the mist."

"I see it! Eliza said, delighting in how the mist settled on her skin.

"They're naturals," Gloria said, wrapping her arms around Kristine. "In another ten years, it could be one of them leading this ride. Imagine that!"

"That's it!" Kristine's eyes lit up.

"What?" Gloria asked.

"I'll show you later, after lunch. If we can get into our cabin after lunch."

"They said it would be ready for us around one, why?"

"Because," Kristine leaned forward to whisper next to Gloria's ear. "I'm kinda wondering if you're still hot and bothered." She nipped Gloria gently, and when she stepped away, she felt Gloria's gaze sweep over her body as she led them back up to the horses, eagerly anticipating when Gloria would be able to explore with her hands instead.

* * *

Gloria was confused when Kristine announced after lunch that it was time the kids headed back to the corral. "You get the keys, and we'll meet back here."

Her heart skipped a beat. "You? Alone?"

"I mentioned to Daisy that the kids want to be guides in training. They are doing the afternoon ride. Without us."

Gloria's gaze fell to Kristine's lips, and she licked her own. "Go! Now!"

"C'mon you two. Saddles are waiting!"

Gloria watched Kristine herd the children back to the corral with the same hip swagger that had driven her crazy ten years ago. Memories of the end of that summer flooded back to her.

She had spent so many nights wondering what Kristine's mouth would feel like on hers. Now she had years of experience, and she could not get the keys to their cabin fast enough.

Waiting for Kristine, she let herself explore all the feelings Kristine's romance had awakened. Being on vacation with no privacy, she had been trying to tamp them down. Now she fanned them to the point that she felt like she would burst when she saw Kristine returning.

Her smile widened with every step she took until she was there, holding Gloria's hand, following her wordlessly to their cabin. Gloria's hand trembled as she worked the unfamiliar lock, but finally it gave, and once they were inside, Kristine had it bolted and Gloria pressed against it.

Kristine's mouth found hers with ferocity. Her tongue pushed inside Gloria's mouth, and Gloria welcomed her, opened wider to pull her deeper. She wrapped her arms around Kristine's back but just as quickly started pulling her shirt from her jeans.

With ease she unclasped Kristine's belt buckle. Kristine pulled off Gloria's T-shirt, followed by her bra, and now her mouth found each budded peak, suckling them as she unfastened Gloria's pants, pushing them past her hips, far enough down that she could catch them with her still-booted foot.

"You still think that old trick will impress me?" Gloria whispered, her entire body pulsing with desire.

"I have new ones," Kristine said wickedly as she knelt before Gloria kissing her soft belly, her hip and then Gloria's center.

Gloria gasped as her lips wrapped around her clit, and she grabbed the door handle with one hand and the back of Kristine's head with the other. "Oh!" She started to lose feeling in her legs as every nerve ending in contact with Kristine's mouth came alive.

Kristine's mouth felt so good.

"I can't…" Her legs were trembling.

"Hmmm?"

The nonverbal question nearly undid Gloria, and a sound she'd never heard before escaped her throat.

And that was before Kristine slipped inside.

How she'd missed the freedom to think of nothing but Kristine's hands on her, coaxing the most delicious agony with every stroke. Higher and higher she climbed until an orgasm shot through her like a bolt of lightning. "I can't…" she panted. Her eyes fluttered open as Kristine stood, her thumb still circling Gloria's throbbing clit. She clung to Kristine's shoulders. "I'm going to fall down!"

"There must be a bed here somewhere."

On nearly useless legs, Gloria stumbled after Kristine who had just enough time to throw back the covers before she fell onto the sheets. "You… Naked… Now…" she panted.

Kristine made quick work of her clothes and was soon poised above Gloria. "You are still so gorgeous, you know that? Hands down the sexiest cowgirl here." She ran her hands down the curves she knew so well, guiding her hips until her center melted into her own. She threw back her head when she felt how wet Kristine was.

"You going to keep me right here?" Kristine asked, grinding against her with just the right pressure.

"For as long as I can. I'm keeping you right here."

Kristine accepted with kisses that matched the motion of her hips, kisses that took Gloria's breath away and stopped when Kristine paused, trembling with release. "That feels so good," she panted as she continued to grind, slowing until she melted against Gloria.

Gloria's hands never left Kristine's skin. So much skin! Her hips, her soft breasts, her strong shoulders. She could not touch enough of it. She felt as if her hands were somehow charging from the contact. "I needed that."

Kristine propped herself up on her elbow. "Yeah, you did."

"I'm not saying that sex fixes everything."

"I know," Kristine chuckled. "But it sure feels good to try."

"I love having sex with you when we're not completely exhausted."

"We've had some long days." Kristine nestled herself back into Gloria's arms. Gloria loved holding Kristine. Nothing in the world compared to it.

"Thank you for bringing us here and for finding a way to ditch the kids so you could have your way with me."

Kristine's hands traced down Gloria's belly, down her right thigh and then back up the left waking new desire. "Even when the trail gets tough, as long as we stay together, I know we'll be fine."

Gloria pushed Kristine onto her back and peppered her with kisses. "The view is always spectacular when it's a challenge to get there."

"We'll find a way to enjoy the view more often, okay?" The way Kristine's eyes traveled the length of her naked body sealed the promise.

Gloria nodded, her throat tight. "I'd be so lost without you," she whispered.

Kristine pulled Gloria close. "There's one thing that you never have to worry about. I always know right where you are."

For a moment, the long list of worries was forgotten and Gloria, herself, knew she was right where she needed to be: in the arms of the woman she loved.

The characters in this short story first appeared in the novels, Take Only Pictures, Such Happiness As This, The Right Thing Easy *and* Cowgirl 101 *by Laina Villeneuve. All of these titles are available from Bella Books or your favorite retailer.*

REACHING OUT

Lise MacTague

KJ winced as she yanked at the exposed corner of the carpet. Adrienne was on a Zoom call, and she didn't want to disturb her girlfriend. She swallowed a curse as the section of carpet hung up on some ancient adhesive. Hopefully the ripping and popping sounds wouldn't be too loud.

"What are you—" Adrienne's voice cut off behind her. She'd seen the chaos of the living room, with half its furniture now in an awkward clump in the middle of the room, and the other half shoved out of the way in the dining room.

"One sec," KJ grunted. She grabbed hold of the carpet's edge and hauled back on it.

"Okay…" Adrienne's lip twitched as she crossed her arms and leaned against the doorframe.

"Goddammit." KJ poked at the thin layer of foam that had adhered to the floor beneath the carpet. That would need to be scraped up.

"KJ, what in god's green earth are you doing?"

"I'm getting rid of the carpet." KJ looked up at her and scrubbed a hand across her forehead. The end of the school year was accompanied by the usual heat. Their house had air conditioning, but given the old Victorian heap's age, it wasn't exactly efficient.

"I can see that," Adrienne said. "Why?"

"It needs to be done." KJ sat back on her heels and considered her meager progress.

"Now?" Adrienne wandered over to the coffee table and perched on the edge. "I agree it needs it eventually, but it's not like anything catastrophic has happened to it lately. Unless there's something you're not telling me."

"I'm sick of staring at it." KJ shrugged. "It's not like I have anything else going on." Carlos had shut down the pub not long after the governor moved the state into the red phase of their COVID response. Carlos had tried to keep his place open for carryout business, but that hadn't been lucrative enough to keep KJ and the other bartender around. And since KJ had been working under the table, she wasn't even eligible for unemployment. She only had a couple of tutoring sessions each week to keep her occupied and to provide a little cash.

"Ah."

"Yeah." KJ winced. "Did I interrupt anything?"

Adrienne shook her head. "Just this week's state of COVID in the district. It's the same as it was last week, and the week before that. I'm sure it'll be the same next week too."

"Only three weeks left to go. That's something."

"It is." Adrienne had been running herself ragged acting as combined tech support and emotional support for her colleagues. Most days she worked from sunup to well after the end of the school day. KJ was sure her girlfriend couldn't wait for the end of the school year. They were so close. The last few months had crawled by.

KJ was doing her best to keep Adrienne freed up during her busy day. She made lunches and dinner, kept an eye on Adrienne's son, and swooped in when their Wi-Fi had issues, but she was still regularly at loose ends.

"I feel so useless. All I'm doing is sitting around and waiting for Lawrence to have a question. That doesn't happen nearly as much as it did back in March. I was trying to figure out what to do today, then I looked over and saw that stain, you know the one that looks like Idaho. I tried to get it out of the carpet, and then I wondered what was under it. One thing led to another and now…" KJ gestured vaguely around the disaster area that had been their living room.

"And now you have a new project." Adrienne got up and walked over to her girlfriend.

KJ opened her arms and enfolded her in a hug. "I don't like sitting around."

"I know." Adrienne squeezed her. "At least we got to finish the hockey season, if barely."

"But no playoffs."

"There's more to life than playoffs." They shared a grin at the refrain. "I'm not surprised you're going stir-crazy. When was the last time you had this much free time on your hands?"

"Oh god." KJ stared up at the ceiling. "I don't think I've ever been this unscheduled. It's awful."

"I bet." Adrienne leaned forward and pressed her lips against her girlfriend's cheek. "I need to get back to my meeting, but we should talk about this. I've been so wrapped up with getting through the end of the year that it didn't occur to me that you might be having issues too."

"It's not your fault," KJ said. "I have a voice. I could have told you."

"Sweetie, you just did." She took a last look at KJ's home improvement project. The carpet had been pulled away from one of the walls. "You've made a good start of it. Promise me you'll stick to the living room?"

"I guess I can do that." The carpeting in the dining room was no better, and then there was the patch in the entry hall that had been worn nearly threadless from person and dog feet coming and going for a decade or two.

"Or at least don't get a bug to redo the office until mid-June."

"I can definitely do that."

"You're the best." Adrienne leaned in for a quick smooch.

The bare brush of her lips still made KJ's heart quicken a year and a half after their first kiss in front of an audience of hundreds.

KJ watched Adrienne make her way to the small bedroom they'd converted to an office for her. It was supposed to be for both of them, but KJ hardly ever used it, except to occasionally print things.

She got back on her knees and continued methodically yanking the carpeting away from the wall. Where the underlay didn't stick, scuffed hardwood was being revealed. She'd hoped it wouldn't be just subfloor beneath and was gratified to be vindicated. The wood was dark with age and would need to be stripped, sanded, stained, and resealed, but it would look amazing once finished.

She glanced toward the small entryway. Adrienne had suggested she stick to the living room, but surely that counted. It was funny, the house was hers—actually, on paper it was her brother's until she paid him his half—but they'd fallen into an easy partnership where the upkeep was concerned. KJ had insisted on paying the bulk of the monthly payment to Erik, which had been working out pretty well between her shifts at Carlos's place and the online tutoring, but the bottom had fallen out of her earnings. *Fucking COVID.*

KJ pulled sharply at a chunk of carpet that was refusing to come up. It didn't budge, so she firmed up her grip on the offending piece and hauled, counting on her body weight to get things moving. It came away all at once. She tried to compensate but ended up landing on her ass.

"Ouch!" It didn't really hurt. The only thing that was bruised was her pride. The whole thing was an apt metaphor for the whole damn situation.

But hey, the carpet was up. Just like, hey, Erik was letting her pay what she could, even if last month that had been nothing.

She grabbed the next section roughly. A carpet tack stabbed through the palm of her work glove.

"Dang it." At the last second, she remembered to keep her voice down. There was no need to bring Adrienne out again. She had enough to worry about without KJ adding to her burdens.

The next piece was easier. She was getting the hang of it, though the tacks were a recurring problem. At least she was able to keep the amount of blood to a minimum.

"What're you doing?" Lawrence's voice pulled her out of the zone a while later.

"Pulling up carpet," KJ said.

He shot her a look identical to the one his mother had given her. KJ made no effort to suppress a grin.

"Really?" Lawrence said. "Did you hear that, Chester?" He looked down at the furry shape by his side. Chester looked up at him with adoring eyes. "It turns out KJ isn't baking a cake like we thought."

"You're hilarious." KJ plopped into a seated position. "I'm refinishing the floor. Look over there." She pointed at one of the cleaner sections that was visible through the tattered underlay. "There's some gorgeous hardwood. Think of how nice it's going to be when this gross old carpet is gone."

"I guess." Lawrence peered at the floor. "It's…nice?"

"It will be." KJ tossed the carpet chunk in her hand onto the growing debris pile in the corner. "You'll see. Do you want to help?"

"Sure!" His face brightened, wiping away the dubious look. "What do I do?"

KJ shifted over to allow him some space, then peeled off her gloves. "Put these on, then grab the edge. All we're doing is removing the carpet layer. Since the foam underneath is almost as gross as the carpeting, it's sticking a bit, so don't worry if it stays behind. And don't worry about tearing it. It's all going to the dump."

Lawrence's eyes sparkled at the prospect of ripping up carpet with abandon. He hauled back on the chunk KJ had indicated. It gave, but not enough to come free, so he set himself more firmly and gave it everything he had. With a loud rip, the carpet shredded along one edge, exposing dark wood and spots of foam.

"That's it," KJ said. She was glad he'd been willing to help. It was nice to have someone to pass this type of stuff on to, but she always asked. Her mom had been the one to do the work around the house. She was at least as handy as Dad had been, but he'd spent a lot of time out of the house making the family extra money on side jobs. These days, KJ was grateful for the skills she'd learned from her mom, but being ordered to help when she wanted to read one more chapter, or do a few more minutes of stickhandling practice, hadn't been her favorite thing. There were times she'd been downright resentful and sulky.

They continued working together, with KJ giving Lawrence tips on what she'd found had been the most effective way to pull up the stubborn flooring. When he had it down, she started scraping the foam away from the wood with a plastic putty knife. It probably would have been easier with a metal one, but she didn't want to scratch the wooden floors.

"You losing steam?" KJ asked when she noticed Lawrence doing as much staring as pulling.

"A bit." Lawrence offered the gloves back to her. "I'm gonna go, okay?"

"Of course. I should probably start figuring out what dinner's going to look like, anyways." She looked around at the carnage of the living room. "I think I've done enough damage."

"Okay," Lawrence said. "I'm gonna go talk to Harper. We're doing superhero drawings of each other."

"Sounds good." KJ's niece had slotted well into Lawrence's small social circle, made even smaller as Adrienne was adamant the family abide by the state's the stay-at-home orders. "Tell her I say hi."

"I will." Lawrence headed for his room. Chester had been watching them from the safety of the dining room, but he popped up and followed his boy. The door closed behind them with a click.

KJ took the time to pile the scrap pieces of carpeting in a corner. She stacked tools and her work gloves on an end table where they'd be easy to find. Her mom had always stressed the importance of neatening up a project site whenever you were ending work for the day. It had been her contention that projects always took longer than you thought because most people failed to factor in prep time and cleanup. KJ tried to keep those things in mind, but she usually wanted to get right to the doing. Some projects took more planning than others.

What would Mom think of this project?

"Huh." She stared at the mess she'd made. Now that was an interesting idea.

* * *

"Are you sure you're ready for this?" Adrienne asked. She was stretched out on the bed, her bare skin dark against the light floral sheets.

KJ ran her nails gently up and down her back. Adrienne arched her back into the contact.

"I haven't spoken to her since I was nine," KJ said. "It's been closer to twenty years than ten. I don't see why I'd wait."

"I don't disagree." Adrienne shivered and goosebumps popped to life on her skin when KJ hit a particularly sensitive spot. "Just know that talking to your mom could bring up some stuff."

"Stuff?" KJ leaned over and dropped a kiss on her shoulder blade.

"Yeah, stuff. It's a technical counseling term."

KJ grinned. "Sounds very clinical."

"I'm not trying to talk you out of this. I think it's a good idea, but I want to make sure you feel like you're ready."

KJ stopped scratched and scooted up behind Adrienne, stretching her body out until her girlfriend was spooned back against her. She loved feeling all of Adrienne's skin against all of hers.

"I am ready," KJ said after a long pause. "At least, I think I am. I mean, I have to find her first, don't I? Once I track her down I can decide whether to reach out or not."

"That's true." Adrienne pulled KJ's arm around her and intertwined their fingers. "I'll be here if you need me."

"I know."

They lay in silence for a long while, listening to the sounds of the house around them. Since the weather had warmed up, the house wasn't as creaky as it was in winter. Through the open window, KJ could barely hear the drone of a neighbor's air conditioner. She was content to lie there with Adrienne and try not worry about what might be coming next, or when she would be getting a steady paycheck again.

"I'm proud of you," Adrienne said after a while of companionable silence. "This is a big step."

"It is." KJ shifted. "But it's not an easy one. Eighteen years is a long time, and my mom's maiden name is pretty common. So is her first name."

"Oh?"

"Susan Davis."

"Oof. Yeah, that's going to be tough. Do you have any idea where she ended up?"

"Not a one. I figured I'd start with a Google search and see if anything comes up in the area." That was about as far as she'd gotten with her plan. If that didn't pan out, she was going to have to figure out something else.

"Well, at least it gives you something to do that isn't an impromptu reno project. I was starting to worry I'd come downstairs to find you knocking out walls to do an open concept thing."

"Har har." KJ nipped her on the shoulder.

Adrienne gasped at the edge to the bite, then again as KJ's fingertips found the ticklish skin along her ribs and burrowed in. She laughed aloud even as she squirmed, trying to get away from those insistent fingers. Soon, her shrieks abated, changing in timbre to something more intimate as KJ gentled her touch and pulled her around for a long, lingering kiss.

* * *

"Dang it!" Even with so mild a curse, KJ still looked guiltily over to Lawrence's room. He was more likely to give her a hard time for swearing than Adrienne was. That had been more effective at curbing her more foulmouthed habits than a lecture from her girlfriend. Not that she'd sworn that much before, but she had become so much more aware of it when there was a kid in the room. Having an eleven-year-old pull out the lecture about curse words while his mom stood nearby and smirked had been effective in getting her to watch her tongue.

Fortunately, Lawrence was unaware of her slip, closed up in his room as he was for the last day of school. She'd lucked out.

Well, in that sense. A promising lead on her mom had turned out to be someone else of the same name and similar age. When KJ had finally found a photo showing this Susan Davis, her heart had fallen. The past few weeks had been filled with similar near-epiphanies. KJ felt like she should have been getting used to the disappointment, but each miss was more frustrating than the one before.

The folks on the phone at the public library had been incredibly helpful in getting her pointed in the right direction, but the task was starting to feel pretty hopeless.

KJ stared at the grainy photo in the terrible copy of a mid-2000s newspaper page. It was probably just as well this wasn't the right Susan Davis. Why would her mom be in Montana anyway?

KJ collapsed back on the couch with a groan. What did she try next? It was amazing how much she didn't know about her mom's family. With more information, she might have been able to work her way back or over from one of them.

"Erik." She sat straight up. Of course! Being five years older than she was, he'd been around for more of Mom's family stories. All KJ could remember was half a story involving a bear and a tree that was hit by lightning. Or maybe the bear had been struck?

She shook her head and pulled out her phone. KJ thumbed open the lock screen. She pulled up his contact info then tapped her finger down on his grinning face, framed on either side by Harper and Emma, her nieces.

As the phone rang, she paced from the couch to the dining room doorway. It rang again as she walked the other way to the front door. By the time he finally answered, KJ had made three circuits of the room.

"KJ," Erik said. "What's going on?" He sounded concerned and distant at the same time.

"Oh shoot," KJ said. "You're working, aren't you?"

"I won't bill the hours to my client, if that's what you're worried about," her brother said dryly.

"Yes, I'm so concerned some massive corporation or rich asshole, I mean jerkwad, is going to owe you an extra fifty bucks."

Erik laughed. "Oh, KJ. That's adorable. Fifty dollars."

"You know what, I don't want to know."

"You really don't." His chair creaked as he shifted position. "So what do you need? If you're willing to give me crap about my rates, it's probably not an emergency."

"Yeah, sorry about that." KJ settled back on the couch. "Time is weird right now, you know?"

"Tell me about it. I feel like I keep losing track of what day of the week it is. Getting groceries delivered lets me know it's Saturday, but I have to keep checking my phone to remind me what day of the week it is."

"We're getting our groceries at the store," KJ said. "There isn't really anyone in town who delivers, though I'm sure some Sussburg teens are making some extra cash by heading down to the GIANT in Harrisburg and dropping things off for the older folks."

"More power to them, then." Erik's chair creaked again. "So what's up?"

"What do you know about Mom's family."

"Mom's family." Erik's voice had gone curiously flat. "Why do you want to know that?"

"Um." That hadn't been the response she'd expected. "Well, I thought it would be good to reach out to her. It's been eighteen years since I last talked to her, you know."

"I know." Erik was quiet for a long moment, then he sighed. "We should talk about it, but this topic really requires a glass of wine. Give me a moment to pour myself one. Maybe a couple."

"I can wait."

"I'm putting you down. I'll be right back."

There was a click as Erik put his phone down, then the sound of footsteps receded quickly. KJ wandered around the living room, taking note of the places where she needed more sanding. Her floor refinishing project had stalled out a little bit once she got all the carpeting and adhesive up, but it still looked so much better than it had. This weekend, she would move the furniture again and finish sanding the hardwood.

It was funny that she still felt like she should wait until the weekend. Without the structure of school or a job, the days melted into one another. Maybe that was why it felt important to differentiate between weekdays and the weekend.

A few minutes later, Erik's voice issued through the phone.

"Okay fine." His voice was the opposite of thrilled. "You want to know about Mom's family so you can try tracking her down, right?"

"Yes." KJ waited for his response, but Erik said nothing. "Why are you being so weird about this? I thought you'd be stoked to talk to her again."

"You'd think." Erik laughed, a low and bitter sound. "Did you know I was supposed to go with her after the divorce?"

"Wait. Really?" KJ cocked her head. That her family's custody arrangement could have been different had never occurred to her.

"Oh yeah. We talked about it. She asked who I wanted to live with and I said her."

"Why would you agree to that?" KJ furrowed her brow. She hadn't had any choice in the matter, it had always seemed to her like she was meant to be with her father.

"We always got on better. Dad and I didn't always see things the same way. We'd started fighting more when I hit middle school. Plus, he seemed way more excited about your hockey than he did about what I was interested in. He tried to act like he cared, but I could tell it was hard. Mom… didn't do that."

"Oh dang." KJ almost whispered the words. "I didn't know any of that. You guys argued a lot, but I figured it was because you were a teenager."

"That was part of it. Mostly, I was so mad that I had to keep living with him. I still don't know why Mom did that. She never said anything to me about it after. The judge basically handed us over to Dad, then we never saw her again."

"That's strange."

"It doesn't matter," Erik said. "She made her choice, and it didn't include me. Or us. It's not like she reached out to us at all, except after Dad died."

"Wait, what?" KJ pulled the phone away from her face and stared at it before returning it to her ear.

Erik laughed bitterly. "Came home after Dad's funeral and there was a message from her on the answering machine. I heard her voice, and just turned it off. Backed the tape up. It was probably recorded over. Doesn't matter. I didn't want to hear what she had to say."

KJ gesticulated with her arms, her mouth working before she was able to put together a coherent sentence. "Jesus Christ, Erik! Don't you think you should have said something to me?"

"I did. You just nodded."

"I nodded at a lot of things. My brain wasn't exactly clicking on all cylinders then. I probably had a hundred thoughts going through my head, and half of them grief." KJ rubbed her eye with the palm of her hand.

"I thought you knew." Erik's voice softened. "I thought you were as mad at her as me. I wasn't exactly thinking straight either."

"I guess." KJ plopped back down on the couch.

"But hey, there is one silver lining to all this."

"What's that?"

"Since you still haven't gotten rid of all of Dad's things, you might have that answering machine."

"True."

"And it's possible the message is still on the tape. It's not like you got a lot of calls to the land line."

"Also true." KJ took a deep breath. "I'll dig around and see if I can track it down. If I do manage to find her, do you want to talk to her?"

"Huh." Erik was quiet. "I need to think about that," he finally said. "Let me know if anything pans out. I'll make a decision then."

"Sounds good." KJ paused, then continued. "I love you, Erik. I'm sorry things shook out how they did with Mom. I'm glad I got to live with you, though."

"Me too." Erik chuckled weakly. "On all accounts. Have a good one, KJ. Say hey to Lawrence and Adrienne."

"Hug the girls for me," KJ said. "Bye now." She reached over and tapped the hang up button. Did she wait until morning or start digging through boxes now?

She shook her head. It could wait. Those boxes had been around for three years. Another night wasn't going to change anything. She had some feelings to sort through.

* * *

KJ stood up straight and pressed her knuckles against the muscles in her lower back. She'd been through two-thirds of the boxes of her dad's stuff that had been relegated to the basement. Her nose itched from a year's worth of dust. Though she'd gotten everything packed up before Adrienne moved in, she hadn't done much more than stick it in the basement.

The boxes of clothes were easy to rummage through. KJ made a mental note to mark those. They could go to the thrift shop when they started taking donations again. That would get rid of a good quarter of the boxes. The rest were full of a random assortment of objects. Those she'd packed up a year ago held things she remembered, but she had no recollection of what was in the first boxes she'd packed away.

That first year after Dad's death had been rough. There were large holes in her memory, swathes of time that had been swallowed up by grief. Those were the boxes she was aiming for. She didn't recall packing up the answering machine. Hopefully that meant it was in a box that had been packed during one of those fugue states, and not that it had already been given away.

At least the basement was cooler than it was upstairs. Early though it was, the day was promising to be a scorcher.

She turned to the next box in the pile. "Kitchen" was scrawled across the side. She considered skipping it, but decided to open it anyway. The box of train pieces had been labeled as living room, which was definitely not where they'd been from.

A mishmash of knickknacks greeted her when she opened the top.

"Ugh." KJ shoved aside a harlequin with a porcelain face and cloth body. She vaguely remembered her dad bringing it back from a trip to New Orleans with the boys. Her mom had hated it, but it had graced one of the living room shelves anyway.

Her hand grazed the corner of something hard and plastic beneath it.

"Is it..." She shoved aside a Bobcats bobblehead and a couple of pucks.

"It is!" KJ extracted the missing machine from the bottom of the box. She held it over her head like a prizefighter's belt for a moment, then headed for the stairs.

"Adrienne," she called out as she took the basement steps two at a time. "I found it!"

Her girlfriend looked up from their tiny kitchen table. A cup of coffee sat in front of her, next to it was a stack of papers. They were probably articles she's found during the school year but was only getting to read now. Her eyes lit up at KJ's excitement.

"Is the tape still inside?" Adrienne asked.

"Oh yeah. Good point." KJ squinted at the answering machine. The old cassette player's window was tinted and difficult to see through, even with the kitchen bright with early morning sunlight. "I think so."

"Plug it in, let's give it a listen." She got out of her chair, giving KJ an easy path to the table and the outlet that lived behind it.

The legs scraped against the floor as KJ pushed it a little too hard in her effort to get the machine plugged in. One prong on the plug was a little bent and it took her a second to get it into the outlet.

KJ placed the answering machine on the table, then stopped.

"Okay." She stared at the square hunk of black and tan plastic.

"Yeah?" Adrienne rested a hand gently on her shoulder, her palm warm through KJ's shirt.

"I'm ready." Despite her words, KJ couldn't make herself press the play button.

"Take your time," Adrienne said. "This is a big moment."

"What is?" Lawrence walked into the kitchen, bleary-eyed from having just woken up. Chester pranced along next to him, toenails clicking merrily on the linoleum.

"KJ is going to listen to a phone message from her mom," Adrienne said.

"That's cool." He eyed the square piece of plastic with suspicion. "On that thing?"

"It's an ancient device known as an answering machine," KJ said. She was dying to know what was on the tape but was grateful to Lawrence for the delay.

"If you say so." He turned to Adrienne. "Can I have some cereal?"

"Of course you can." She pointed at the cabinet behind him. "You know where the bowls are."

"Yeah." His jaws stretched in a large yawn.

"You should eat in the dining room. I think KJ has dibs on the kitchen table."

"Okay." He headed toward the fridge.

KJ went back to staring at the machine. She took a deep breath, then reached out and pressed play.

The machine clicked to life and the hiss of the tape came out of the small speaker. KJ cocked her head, listening intently for anything that might resemble her mom's voice.

"It's blank," she said, her voice quiet.

"Maybe Erik didn't rewind it," Adrienne said. She squeezed KJ's shoulder gently.

"He said he did." KJ covered her girlfriend's hand with her own. She chewed on her lower lip as she rewound the tape, then pressed play again.

The tape whirred to life once more. A short burst of static issued from the speaker, then was followed by a high-pitched beep.

"Hello?" The sound quality wasn't great, but there was no mistaking KJ's mom's voice. KJ stood up, not noticing when the chair hit the floor with a clatter. "This is…Mom." Her voice trailed off for a moment. "I saw the obituary about Dad. I'm so very sorry for your loss. Both of you." Her voice firmed as she expressed her condolences. "Please call me. I'd love to talk to you. My number is—" KJ whirled around, looking frantically for paper and pen, but Adrienne was already pressing it into her hands. "—617-848-2211. Please." KJ's eyes filled with tears as her mom's voice broke, or maybe that was a hiccup in the tape. "Call me. It's been too long."

The message ended.

"She sounded sad," Lawrence said. He leaned against the counter, his cereal bowl forgotten in the tiny drama that was unfolding at the small table with its chipped top.

"You think so?" KJ rubbed her eyes.

"Are you gonna call her?"

Adrienne raised her eyebrows, echoing her son's question.

"I think so." Was she really? "I am." It had been so long. Was there a better time? It had been months since they'd seen Adrienne's folks. She often thought about Moesha and Levar, and knew that Adrienne was worried sick about them. They were both in decent health, but Levar had some high blood pressure issues.

Neither of them had any problem masking up, thankfully. Justus had given Carleton an earful about not being careful about his own mask wearing after he'd moved back home when his university had shifted to online classes. Since the lecture from his older brother, he'd been better, but KJ suspected it was more to keep his siblings off his back than because he had any real concern regarding the virus.

How was her mom? She was hitting the age range where COVID was a concern. Was she taking care of herself? Could she afford to have groceries delivered? Had she already gotten sick and passed away?

"I have to call her." KJ reached for her phone.

"What about Erik?"

KJ stopped at Adrienne's soft question. She had promised to let him know before she called.

"I should…" Her voice trailed off. What should she do? She'd promised, but now that she'd heard her mom's voice, her fingers practically trembled with the effort of not punching in the numbers that were scrawled on the paper in front of her. He didn't even want to talk to Mom. Erik was the one who'd chosen to keep her in the dark.

But he didn't erase the message.

"Yeah, I'll call him." She swiped open her phone and scrolled through her recent calls. She stabbed a finger down on his number then waited. The phone rang a few times, then went to voice mail.

"Hey, it's me." KJ took a deep breath. "I found the answering machine and the tape with her message on it. I have her number. Let me know ASAP if you want to be on the call." She hung up, then stared at the screen for a second. For good measure, she texted him the same message.

When he didn't respond right away, KJ looked up at Adrienne.

"Where's the 617 area code?"

* * *

"Are you ready?" KJ asked her brother.

"Maybe we should give her a heads-up first," Erik said.

"Maybe so." KJ shrugged, though Erik wouldn't be able to see it through the phone. "If we have to leave a message, that's not the end of the world, is it?"

"I guess not." KJ could hear shuffling sounds through their connection. She imagined he was pacing around his office. The need to move when anxious was definitely a family trait. Did Mom share it?

"I'm doing it," she said firmly. "We'll handle whatever comes of it."

"Yeah, okay."

"Give me a second while I see if I can add her to the call." KJ pulled the phone away from her ear before Erik could raise a new objection. She glanced at the scrap of paper with their mom's number on it, then typed it in. Hopefully technology would do its thing and add their mom to their call.

The phone rang.

"It's ringing," Erik said.

"Oh good." Her tone was dry, but she was glad to know Erik could hear what was going on.

The call buzzed down through the line to them again.

"Who answers unknown calls anymore?" Erik fretted.

"Dad did. She's from the same generation, so maybe she never got over the burning need to answer a ringing phone either."

The phone rang a third time.

"Then why isn't she picking up?"

"I don't know," KJ said. "We're working with the same amount of information here."

"I know. It's just—"

"Hello?" The woman's voice broke in to their worried bickering.

KJ waited for Erik to say something, but the line was quiet. She gave it a beat, figuring he should be the one to open the conversation, but he stayed silent.

"Hello." The questioning tone in that oh-so-familiar voice sharpened to annoyance.

"Hi Mom," KJ said.

"Mom, it's me," Erik said at the same time.

KJ shut her mouth, not wanting to squelch her brother's time with their mom, but Erik stopped talking at the same time.

"Erik?" Emotion throbbed behind her utterance of his name. "Kristjana?"

"She's still going by KJ," Erik said. "But yeah, it's us."

"Hello," KJ said.

"Oh my god." There was a long pause. "It's really you? My babies. Erik and KJ." Her voice sharpened again. "What's wrong? Why are you calling now? Are you both all right? None of you is sick, are you? Your wife and children are all right, Erik?"

"We're fine," KJ said when the silence threatened to reestablish itself. "I thought it was time to reach out. I didn't know…" She trailed off, not sure how to tell their mom that her son had hidden her attempt at reaching out three years ago.

"I got your message, Mom," Erik said. "I didn't tell KJ."

"I see." Their mom sighed. "I understand."

"She was trying to track you down."

"Trying and failing," KJ said. "Susan Davis isn't exactly the most uncommon name in the world."

Their mom laughed, a warm sound that transported KJ back to the good times before her parents started sniping at each other. Before they split and she started coming home to a nearly empty house after school each day.

"Well, you wouldn't have found me that way anyway," her mom said. "It's Susan Chatterjee now."

"Oh," Erik said, his voice too bright, "you remarried."

"I did. A number of years ago now, then legally in 2015."

The year 2015. That meant something. KJ's head snapped up. "You're married to a woman?"

"I am." Her voice was quiet. "Is that a problem for you two?"

Erik laughed, the sound an odd mixture of surprise and relief.

"Um, no," KJ said. "I guess I come by it honestly, then."

"That's for sure," Erik said. "KJ's not married, but she is living in sin with an amazing woman."

"That's fantastic!" Their mom's voice lit up. "How long have you been together? What does she do for a living? Are you going to marry her? Tell me everything."

KJ opened her mouth to do exactly that, but closed it when Erik spoke first.

"We wouldn't have to tell you everything if you'd stuck around. I get that you and Dad divorced. It makes more sense now that we know you're with a woman. But why? Why did you ask me who I wanted to live with if you weren't going to take me with you? Why?" He inhaled sharply after the last plaintive word.

"Oh, Erik." Their mom's voice was as pained as her son's. "I wanted to. I wanted to so much, but…"

"But what?" Erik's voice raised to just below a shout. "What was so much more important than me?"

"Erik…" KJ said. "Maybe cool it a bit?"

"It's all right, KJ. He deserves to know. I wish I could see you both in person, to explain." She laughed, her voice bitter. "But it seems I can't do that right now either. Erik, this is going to be hard to hear. Are you sure you want to know?"

"Yes."

"It was your dad. He…he wasn't happy when I told him I was leaving him. The separation period was difficult, especially since I was still in town."

"I remember that," KJ said. It had been an awkward time. Their mom would be home after school. She would spend time with them and make dinner, but then would leave a few minutes before their dad usually got home from work.

"I met someone while we were living apart," their mom continued. "She was wonderful, and I felt like I was me again, in a way I hadn't for a long time." She paused. "He didn't take it well. He was so mad that I was leaving him, then got even angrier when he decided I was leaving him for a woman. I wasn't. I met her after we broke up, but that didn't change his mind."

"Did your new girlfriend not want a teenager hanging around?" Erik asked, his voice sharp.

"That was never a consideration," their mom said. "I made it perfectly clear we were a package deal. No, Dale didn't want you or KJ exposed to my 'filth,' I believed he called it. He hired a PI and got photos of me with Lisa. It was a big to-do in court when he unveiled them to the judge. That old bastard was as right wing as they come and he terminated my parental rights. Called me unfit."

"Dad did that?" Erik whispered. "That can't be right."

"I don't know, Erik," KJ said. "It's not that far off." He'd never been homophobic to her, had never yelled at her or threatened her for being who she was, but he hadn't been thrilled about the idea. KJ had only brought one girlfriend home while he was alive. The experience had been so awkward that she hadn't repeated it. When he'd been sick with Alzheimer's, she definitely hadn't wanted to bring anyone into that.

"He was very, very angry," their mom said. "I had no idea he'd be that upset. If I had…"

"Jesus, Mom," Erik said. "There wasn't any way you could have snuck over, or…"

"If I'd been caught, they could have sent me to jail. How would that have helped? They couldn't stop me from sending letters and cards, though."

"We didn't get those," KJ said.

"I'm not surprised." Their mom took a deep breath, then continued, a forced cheerfulness in her voice. "You need to tell me all about what's going on with your lives. I have so much catching up to do. And then when this is all over, I want to see you. And your families. And you can meet mine."

"Are you all right?" KJ asked. "Haven't gotten sick? How are the rates in Boston?"

"Not great, but we're doing better than New York."

"That's a relief. Sussburg is getting by pretty unscathed. Adrienne and I are being cautious, though."

"Sophie doesn't let me out the front door without mask, gloves, and hand sanitizer," Erik said.

"I'm glad to hear it," their mom said. "It's been a challenge, for sure."

Their conversation trickled into nothing.

"So when can we talk again?" KJ asked. "I know you want to hear everything, but I'm sure this hasn't been the afternoon you thought it was going to be."

"And I want to see you," their mom said. "It won't be the same, but if we can talk on the computer, it'll be better than nothing. Way more satisfying than only seeing KJ through the cage of a helmet."

KJ beamed. "You caught my games?"

"Of course I did. Hockey still isn't my favorite thing, but I never missed a Quinnipiac U game when you were playing. I knew something was wrong when you stopped halfway through the season. I was able to reach out to some folks I still know in the area, which is when I found out Dale wasn't doing well."

Time to change the subject, KJ thought. "We're all about Zoom these days. We can hook up there if you want."

"I do want."

"Us too," Erik said. "You can meet your granddaughters."

"I'm so glad." Their mom's smile came through the phone. "We'll talk tonight?"

"Of course," KJ said. "There's nothing I'd rather do."

"It's not like we're going out these days," Erik said.

"Good. It's a date. I love you both very much, and I can't wait to find out everything I missed."

"I love you too, Mom," KJ said.

"Love you," Erik said quietly.

"Tonight," she repeated. "Call at six. Text your email addresses to this number, and I'll get a room set up for us."

"Yes, Mom," KJ and Erik chorused, and then her end of the call went dead.

"That was a lot," Erik said after a moment.

"It was," KJ replied. "But not too much, I don't think."

"No, but it did give me a lot to consider. I'll see you tonight, KJ."

"See ya." She hung up the phone and swiped over his image, ending the call. The app closed, leaving her staring at her and Adrienne's faces grinning up at her through a screen of app icons.

It had been good to hear Mom's voice again. She hadn't realized how much she'd missed it until she heard it again. There was so much she'd missed in her mom's life, and so much their mom had missed in theirs.

Well, she had the time, and she was finally putting it to good use.

The characters in this short story first appeared in the novel Breaking Out *by Lise MacTague.* Breaking Out *is available from Bella Books or your favorite retailer.*

THE EYES HAVE IT

Catherine Maiorisi

"Damn it, Zoe. Life is about more than serving ourselves."
I pushed away from the table in disgust. "Haven't you seen the
news, seen all those nurses and doctors in New York City going
to work every day despite how exhausted and overwhelmed they
are? I *have* to go."

She cupped her ear. "Do I hear your hero complex speaking?"

I ignored the contempt I'd been noticing more and more
lately. "I became a nurse to help people. And that's what I'm
going to do."

"Even though New Yorkers consider us Idahoans yokels?"
She met my gaze. "You're pathetic."

I am pathetic. Why else would I still be with her? I'd avoided
examining our relationship, afraid what I'd see. But I could no
longer deny that whatever attraction or love had brought us
together no longer existed.

Zoe leaned back, as if considering the situation, as if she had
a voice in this decision. "Well…the money does sound good. We
won't have to worry about making the mortgage payment and

other expenses." She flashed the sweet, self-deprecating smile she always used to deflect my pressing her to pay her share. "And maybe you'll stop nagging me about money."

For once I spoke before my filter could mute my response. "We wouldn't have to worry about expenses if you didn't spend most of your paycheck on yourself, on your…entertainment."

The wounded look that replaced her smile used to melt my heart and always resulted in me backing down. But this time was different. I wasn't feeling remorse, or the usual sadness, and definitely not love. I was angry and disgusted with her. And myself.

Zoe looked away. It didn't mean she was embarrassed. She was giving me time to feel bad and apologize. Not this time. I left the kitchen and went into our bedroom. Or more accurately my bedroom since she'd claimed my hours disturbed her sleep and moved into the guest room a few months ago. I took down my suitcase and began to pack. When I turned back to the closet, Zoe was watching from the doorway. "What are you doing?"

"Like I said, I'm driving to New York tomorrow morning with Lottie and two other nurses."

"You made this decision without discussing it with me?" She sounded incredulous. "How long have you known?"

I met her eyes. "Ten days. Maybe if you'd been home when I was awake instead of god knows where, I would have talked to you about it."

"What am I supposed to do? Stay home alone for two weeks while you work the night shift? And then stay home with you when you work your two weeks of days?"

Always the victim. Why had it taken me so long to notice? "Well let's see. Since I'm basically supporting us, you could try to make my life a little easier. Instead you expect me to shop, cook dinner for us, clean the house and do your wash whatever shift I'm working. It would be nice if you did some of those things some of the time. And, oh, maybe you could stay home occasionally so we could be together."

Zoe cleared her throat. "I have to go. I have plans tonight. How long will you be away?"

Did she even care? "Thirteen weeks."

She shrugged. "Have a safe trip."

I stared at the empty doorway.

After a sleepless night, I was out of bed at five-fifteen. I checked the second bedroom. Zoe hadn't come home last night. Again. Why hadn't I let myself see the truth? The sex was good in the beginning. I thought it was love but it was probably lust. Maybe it was the same for her. But we'd never developed the emotional connection necessary for a loving adult relationship and we'd drifted apart. It wasn't all her fault though. I found it easier to let things slide than argue. Instead of breaking up I'd allowed Zoe to become dependent and we'd shifted into a parent-child dynamic. I sighed. I couldn't do anything about it now but I'd deal with this…situation when I returned.

At six on the dot, Artie's SUV pulled up with Ginny in the front passenger seat. I greeted them and climbed into the back with my best friend Lottie. She studied me as she handed over the latte and the egg and cheese sandwich she'd picked up for me. Once we were speeding along the highway, she spoke so only I could hear. "Trouble in paradise?"

I nearly choked on the latte. "I wouldn't know, it's been a long time since I've been there."

"That bad?" I looked away. Lottie touched my arm. "I'm sorry Annie. I know I've said it before but you really deserve better."

In the past, I'd jumped to Zoe's defense when Lottie said that very thing. But now I was done with her. I blinked to hold back the tears, not for the lost relationship but for how little value I'd placed on myself. I deserved a loving, supportive partner and a relationship of equals. And I'd find it. "I'm over her. I don't want to leave the house empty for three months but I'm going to ask her to move out when I return."

Lottie grinned. "I'm so happy for you I won't even say I told you so."

We'd signed on as traveling nurses because it was the fastest way to get assigned to a hospital and we were scheduled to start work in five days. According to Google Maps it would take thirty-eight hours to drive the two thousand five hundred miles to New York City but rather than drive straight through and be exhausted when we arrived, we planned to drive nine hundred miles a day and sleep two nights in motels.

Artie's SUV was comfortable; we alternated drivers and stopped every three hours to stretch, pee, and pick up snacks or lunch. When I wasn't driving I had plenty of time to think. And as we passed signs along I-90 for Mount Rushmore in South Dakota, Devils Tower in Wyoming and Witches Gulch in Wisconsin, my long-forgotten dreams kept floating to the surface. I'd planned to get nursing experience, travel around America and Europe and Asia, then join a group like Doctors Without Borders to help others. I'd become a nurse practitioner and acquired the extra skills that would help me work almost anywhere but somewhere along the way I let my dreams slip away. No wonder Zoe found me boring. As I considered my life, I found myself boring. This trip to New York City was the first out of my comfort zone but I vowed it wouldn't be the last.

The day in April we arrived was one of the worst days of the Pandemic. New York City felt like a post-apocalypse city. The streets were deserted. And the quiet was freaky. We had no trouble finding parking near the New Yorker Hotel where we would be staying with hundreds of other volunteer nurses and doctors from all over the country. The next day I was assigned to Elmhurst Hospital, the absolute worst hot spot in the city, while my three friends were assigned to other hospitals.

I was nervous and excited about what was to come and had no trouble getting up at five to make the six-fifteen a.m. charter bus that would deliver me and the other personnel assigned to Elmhurst. I dressed, threw a couple of masks in a plastic bag, grabbed a bite to eat, and headed to the front of the hotel to board the bus. During the ride to Queens the new people like me, fresh and raring to go, chatted and commented on the sights but the others who clearly had been working at the hospital for a while were quiet and withdrawn, either staring straight ahead or sleeping.

When we arrived in front of the hospital new people were directed to get their assignments from the two people standing in front of the tent outside the ER. Outfitted in full PPE and holding an iPad, they were easy to spot. The guy keyed in my name. "You'll be working in the ICU on the fifth floor, Annie." He handed me a sealed plastic bag. "Put on your protective gear. The surgical mask goes over the N95." I did as instructed and slipped on the shoe booties, protective gown, plastic face shield, and gloves. When I finished he nodded his approval. "Follow the green line straight through the ER to the elevators. Don't forget the bus back to your hotel leaves from here at seven-fifteen sharp. If you miss it, you'll have to take a taxi."

They'd erected the tent to keep non-critically ill patients out of the emergency room and away from risk so walking through the Emergency Room I felt like I'd somehow ended up in a war zone. No blood but coughing, gasping, moaning critically ill patients stacked in every available space and the limited staff moving quickly to treat them.

On the fifth floor, the war zone atmosphere in the ER seemed peaceful compared to the Intensive Care Unit. Machines beeping, people moaning, orders being voiced, telephones ringing, it was noisy as hell. And with equipment everywhere, and gowns and gloves strewn about, it was messy. The tension was palpable. My eyes wide and my mouth hanging open, I finally understood what controlled chaos meant. I'd never seen so many terribly sick patients jammed together but it was the number of intubated patients that stopped me short. How did these people work under these conditions? How do they monitor so many patients? How do they stay on top of the medications needed?

"Annie McCallum?" I heard my name but I couldn't look away from the disaster in front of me. A hand gripped my shoulder. "Annie."

I blinked and looked into kind eyes that seemed to be smiling but it could have been the lights reflecting off the plastic shield worn by Dr. Rory Wade. That was the name scrawled across the headband of the person standing in front of me reading the ID dangling from my neck. Several inches taller than my five-eight and with a deep voice, Dr. Wade could be a man or a woman but with the N95 and surgical mask, the plastic shield and the rest of the PPE, I couldn't tell. The doctor put both hands on my shoulders and turned me so we were face-to-face. "I know it's shocking but you'll get used to it. Do you think you can focus enough to help?"

I took a deep breath. "Of course, Dr. Wade. Sorry. It's just—"

"I know." The doctor squeezed my shoulder. "Come." Dr. Wade led me to the locker room. "First, your ID goes under your PPE. Second store your bag."

When I was ready, the doctor escorted me to a group preparing to prone a patient. It was backbreaking work for the staff but being on his stomach would help him breathe easier. "Folks, this is Annie. She's all yours." Dr. Wade turned to me. "See you later, Annie." A woman standing at the head of the bed tipped her head at me. "Make room for Annie and let's get this done." I moved to the empty spot and we flipped the patient onto his stomach. While the others tended to him, I stepped back, unsure where I was needed next.

"Annie." The nurse who had directed the move was at my side. "I'm Gracie, the head nurse. Give me a quick rundown of your experience."

When I finished, her eyes crinkled which I think meant she was smiling. "Wow. An acute care nurse practitioner also trained as a nurse anesthetist and certified for medical transport. So you have experience intubating?"

"I do." I was proud. "I work in the ER in a small rural hospital in Idaho so we don't always have an anesthesiologist available. And we often transport patients by air to big city hospitals so I've trained to do what's needed."

"I'm going to buy a lottery ticket tonight, just in case my luck holds." Gracie turned. "Follow me."

And so it began. Of course, being conscientious, Gracie didn't take my word for my experience. "Dr. Montgomery, this is Annie McCallum. She's an Acute Care Nurse Practitioner and she'll be doing intubations when you leave so I need you to work as a team." She turned to me. "Dr. Montgomery is our anesthetist but her two-week stint ends in three days."

"Three days?" I couldn't keep the panic out of my voice. Gracie patted my arm. "Don't worry. You won't be alone. I'm also certified and Dr. Wade will work with us."

Actually, I was fine doing the work, had done it in the ER and the OR as required, but though the ER at home was a high-pressure environment it was nothing like the roiling crisis in this ICU with so many incredibly sick patients needing intense care. We intubated three patients together then Dr. Montgomery observed as I did two. After that we worked separately. Three people died in the ICU that day. I was holding the hand of a frightened patient, trying to calm and comfort her when Gracie reminded me it was seven o'clock. I had no idea it was so late. I went to the locker room to get my plastic bag and store my masks for tomorrow.

Dr. Wade walked in. "I have a gift for you, Nurse McCallum. I didn't realize you'd be primarily intubating or I would have given it to you earlier."

"Thank you." I could have kissed the good doctor. Putting a ventilator tube down the throat of patients as sick as we were treating exposes you to aerosol droplets of the virus. I hoped the double masks would be enough protection. But the Powered Air-Purifying Respirator has a hood that goes over your head to your shoulders and uses a battery-operated blower to move contaminated air though a filter that removes toxic virus particles. I smiled as I put it in the locker. "I was worried about doing intubations with just the masks and plastic shield but I assumed the hospital didn't have any PAPRs."

"I found a few hidden away, probably from their bioterrorism training. It can be cleaned and reused so don't let it out of your sight." She walked me to the elevator. "Goodnight."

My gut feeling that Dr. Wade was a woman was confirmed as I watched her move gracefully through the tumult of the ICU, an island of calm in a torrential storm. I felt a ping of attraction. Interesting.

As Dr. Wade predicted, I barely noticed the hectic environment the next day. In my years as a trauma nurse, I'd experienced some very intense times in the ER after pileups, plane crashes or shootings but they usually eased up after a few hours. At Elmhurst, in the middle of the pandemic, the pressure, the intensity never let up. We were up against an enemy we'd never seen before and really had no idea how to defeat. It was crisis after crisis, a relentless battle to save lives, to fight despite feeling overwhelmed, to not lose hope despite the deaths. We worked 12-hour shifts for 21 days straight before getting a day off. I was exhausted at work but when my day off came I felt guilty and unable to enjoy the things I'd been looking forward to like napping, reading, and exercising. Understaffed and up against shortages of basic needs like N95 masks, other PPE and essential ventilators, there was always more to do, more patients to care for. We were all stretched thin: even specialists were performing medical procedures they hadn't done in years and helping out with necessary nonmedical tasks like transporting patients. And despite the danger of the virus, the cleaning staff, unseen and unheralded, disinfected beds and rooms as patients died or left the unit, emptied trash bins and washed floors.

I'd never worked in such a grim environment with so few successes. I'd seen patients die. I'd had patients die on me. But I'd never seen death in this magnitude. Seeing the fear in their eyes when we told patients they had to be intubated was excruciating. But the hardest part was watching them die alone. When we could we held their hands and comforted them, helped them connect with family by phone or video, but it was never enough. They died without family around them and sometimes we didn't even have the time to let their loved ones know they were dying or inform them that they'd died. On the day I saw bodies being moved into the refrigerated trucks brought in to hold the dead because the morgues were filled, I thought I'd break. But I went on. We all did. And then when a patient who seemed to be getting better took a sudden turn for the worse and died before we could react, I cracked. Dr. Wade held me while I cried, then led me away for a quiet cup of coffee in the closet she'd appropriated as her office. She encouraged me to talk about my feelings and acknowledged how difficult this was for all of us. As we exchanged a little personal information I realized that though I'd touched patients and held their hands, I hadn't been held since long before I came to New York. It felt good. The softness of her breasts and her scent sparked something in me that I hadn't felt in a very long time and I suddenly saw her in a different light. To my surprise she held my hand, her thumb brushing gently and even through our protective gloves my body responded with a surge of warmth. Something seemed to have shifted for her as well. She didn't let go of my hand during the fifteen minutes we were in her intimate space. Perhaps she needed the contact too.

When I returned to the unit I was administering meds with Gracie and I noticed Dr. Wade quietly talking with a patient. It occurred to me that she was always comforting patients and staff. "Who takes care of Dr. Wade? Who comforts her?" I wasn't aware I'd said it aloud until Gracie answered. "Good question. I don't know how she does it. She comes in early in the morning and stays late at night to soothe patients, and she does the same for all of us. I've never known such a caring and loving doctor." Gracie glanced at me. "You know they all start out wanting to help people but somewhere along the way, probably medical school, many of them build a barrier between them and the rest of us. In some cases, it's to protect themselves from feelings, in other cases they acquire a God complex and think they're above us all."

I did know. I'd encountered all types of doctors in my work, but none as empathetic and seemingly as dedicated as Dr. Rory Wade. She intrigued me. Though I had never seen her without her PPE and had no idea of what she looked like, her eyes and her voice were in my head constantly, especially in the quiet at night when I was alone in bed. After that intimate few minutes together I became aware that Rory, as I began to think of her, touched me a lot during the day. The pats on the back, squeezes of the arm and occasional shoulder massages weren't sexual, they just provided normal human contact in the middle of the tsunami of death. At least as normal as it could be while swathed in PPE as we both were. I really liked it. And longed for more. I also noticed that we gravitated to one another and often ended up working with the same patient, intubating, proning, monitoring, and medicating. We talked while we worked. She asked questions about my life and over time I shared the name of the hospital I worked at, that I co-owned my house with the bank, and I was leaving a bad relationship with a woman.

As the days flew by things got worse, not better, and driven to save as many people as I could, I started putting in longer hours. It was an impossible task. I frequently stayed after my shift to hold the hand of a dying patient. And occasionally to hold a phone or an iPad so a patient could talk to family or a family could see their dying loved one. Rory and I frequently gravitated to the same bed, trying to ease or comfort a patient. And if our hands touched it was comforting, even with double gloves. More than once I fell asleep in a chair at a patient's bedside and she sent me home in a taxi. I never thought to question why if we both worked the seven to seven shift she was always there when I arrived and still there when I left.

I didn't want to leave Elmhurst but I knew I couldn't continue at this pace. When I mentioned my dilemma to Rory she convinced me to go home for a couple of months, then sign up again. So three weeks before my contract was up, I had a long phone conversation with Zoe. I told her I was through and asked her to be out of my house by the time I got home. She tried to charm me and when I didn't relent, she actually apologized for the way she'd treated me. It was nice to hear but I wasn't sure if she meant it or it was just a ploy to get me to change my mind. In the end, she agreed to bring in a cleaning company a few days before I returned and be gone when I arrived home. I was dubious.

With two weeks left, I started feeling sick. It started with a terrible headache. I was tired all the time so I didn't notice my extreme fatigue. I chose to attribute my shortness of breath to lack of exercise. Then one afternoon I started coughing and my temperature spiked. I was afraid to face what I knew with certainty. I had contracted COVID-19. I felt weak. My brain was foggy. And when I was called to intubate a patient I had to admit I wasn't fit to do it. "Gracie, I can't—" Gasping for breath, I collapsed into Gracie's arms.

"I need help here," Gracie said, a note of panic in her usually calm voice.

Before I could freak, I heard Dr. Wade's steady voice. "I've got you, Annie." I felt myself being lifted and moved through space. "Oxygen, now." Dr. Wade's voice was calm as she issued crisp orders. I felt air on my face as the plastic shield was replaced by an oxygen mask, felt the gentle touches as my clothes were stripped off. A hand gently brushed my hair off my forehead. "Annie, it's Dr. Wade. Do I have your permission to intubate you?"

I knew what that meant. Only a small percentage of our patients made it off a ventilator alive. But even with oxygen I was struggling to breathe. I didn't want to suffocate. I had enough brain space left to know I had no choice. "Yes." I gazed into her eyes, not sure whether I'd said it or thought it. Her nod to Gracie who was hovering nearby confirmed I'd said it. "Please don't let me die, Rory." And then, even in my panic, in my struggle to maintain clarity, I knew it wasn't fair to make her feel responsible for my life. I gasped. "Just do your best, that's enough."

Dr. Wade held my gaze. "I promise to do everything I can. I'll be with you all the way, Annie, but you have to do your part. You're young and you're strong, promise me you'll fight as hard as you can." I nodded. "Is there someone we should call?"

"Lottie. Phone." She said something but I didn't hear what. As she faded, I understood they'd sedated me to insert the tube.

During the seven days I was on the ventilator, I was aware of being flipped often, my hand being held and people talking to me. Once unhooked, I took another two days to slowly come out of the sedation. As my brain fog lifted, I realized I hadn't seen Rory since I woke. "Gracie, where is Dr. Wade?"

Gracie cleared her throat. "Dr. Wade personally managed your case. She monitored you constantly, spent as much time with you as she could during her shift and slept in a chair next to your bed every night, all the while holding your hand and talking to keep you tethered to the world. She gave her all to ensure your recovery."

I waited but she didn't continue. "So why haven't I seen her?"

"She collapsed the day after we removed you from the ventilator. You know how driven she is? I think you being so sick put her over the edge and everything finally caught up with her."

I looked around the ICU. "Is she here?"

"No, hon, she doesn't have COVID, so we had to move her off the floor. I understand her partner, who is also a doctor, picked her up and took her home to care for her."

Tears stung my eyes. I hadn't realized she had a partner. "Did she leave a message for me?"

"No. I'm sorry. She wasn't conscious when she was moved off the unit." Gracie gave me a moment to take that in. "She did call Lottie to let her know you were sick. I've spoken to Lottie. She wants to FaceTime with you to talk about getting you home."

They kept me a few more days to make sure I didn't relapse and in further conversations with Gracie I learned that while I was on the ventilator my colleagues had regularly volunteered extra time to help flip me, a complicated process with someone on a ventilator, and sit with me so someone was always holding my hand and talking to me.

Gracie helped me dress then eased me into a wheelchair. I cried when my colleagues clapped and wished me well as Gracie rolled me through the ICU to the elevator. Lottie and Artie were waiting outside but the three of us resisted the urge to hug. Apparently Ginny, our fourth passenger, had given up halfway through the contract so it would be just the three of us. Our suitcases were strapped on top of the SVU so I could be stretch out on the rear seat they'd arranged with blankets and pillows. Gracie helped me into the car. And we were off to Idaho. Artie and Lottie split the driving. I mostly slept or quietly mourned the loss of Rory.

I stayed with Lottie for a week when we got back, then she returned to work and I went home to my clean, empty house. I could dress and feed myself but I couldn't do much else so Lottie, Artie, and other friends came for lunch or dinner and brought food. But after three months of intense focus, three months with a mission, three months being part of a team dealing with life and death many times each day, I felt lost and lonely. And though I knew it wasn't healthy, I missed Rory. It was weird that I couldn't even put a face to my fantasies.

Lottie and Artie had trouble settling back into a normal hospital environment and were frustrated trying to get our colleagues to understand what we'd been through. Although I was ostensibly over the virus and had no lung, heart or cognitive symptoms or any musculoskeletal impairment from the proning, doing the simplest things exhausted me. Lottie and I devised a rehab program that started with lots of rest and healthy food then gradually added exercise. By mid September, two months after getting home, I had enough stamina to return to the ER part-time days only.

By the end of September, I was back full-time and we were seeing more COVID-19 cases each day. One day in early October I was with a very sick patient in her late twenties who we'd diagnosed with COVID-19. She was frightened and gasping for breath. I tried to reassure her by sharing that I'd survived the virus and promised to visit her. As she was wheeled off to the ICU, I ran to the locker room, threw off my PPE, washed up, then ran outside to get myself together. I wouldn't last long in the ER if I couldn't control my emotions. At the entrance to the ER I took deep breaths trying to soothe myself. I was surprised to see Lottie chatting with someone a few yards away. I couldn't see the person she was talking to or make out the words but my body reacted to the voice. Dr. Rory Wade? Was I having some kind of flashback?

Lottie noticed me. "Annie."

The other woman turned. We locked eyes. She smiled. I'd never seen her without the PPE, never seen her face, but I'd recognize those piercing dark eyes anywhere. I'd fallen in love with her humanity, her kindness, her gentleness, with who she is rather than what she looked like. But she was as beautiful on the outside as she was on the inside. Tall and confident, as I remembered, with short dark hair, cream-colored skin, and a lovely smile. She seemed to glow.

"Look who I found wandering around looking for you." I heard Lottie's voice from a distance.

I couldn't take my eyes off her as she walked to me. "Doctor Wade." It was all I could say.

"Hey. It's Rory. Remember?" She grinned. "You look a lot better than the last time I saw you."

I laughed. "I feel a lot better. What are you doing here?"

Lottie put a hand on each of our shoulders. "Um, I hate to break this up, ladies, but you're blocking the entrance to the ER. How about you two go out for lunch and talk. I'll cover for you Annie. Take your time."

I led Rory across the street to the diner. We grabbed a table and sat staring at each other. Gloria, the waitress, cleared her throat. "Hi Annie, ready to order."

"A cup of coffee, a grilled cheese sandwich, and a bowl of tomato soup." I'd been eating a lot of comfort food recently and this was my favorite lunch. Gloria probably put the order in when she saw me walking across the street.

Gloria looked at Rory.

"I'll have the same."

We gazed at each other. Rory reached across the table and took my hands in hers. My body reacted as it usually did to contact with her and the diner suddenly felt tropical. But she had a partner and I wasn't about to have an affair. I leaned back and released her hands. "I heard you collapsed and your, um, partner took you home to nurse you back to health."

"Actually former business partner. Emily is my best friend and the closest thing I have to family so she's my emergency contact. When I collapsed they called her. She and her wife Lillian drove to Queens to get me and took me to their home to care for me."

"Oh, when I heard partner, I assumed you were lovers." I put my hands on the table, palm up.

Rory smiled and captured my hands again. "We were lovers in medical school but by the time we opened our medical practice in Pennsylvania our relationship was over."

"Former business partner? What happened?"

"I acknowledged that our lucrative practice wasn't meeting my needs, that I wanted to use my medical skills to help the people who need it most. So in January Emily and I agreed to end the partnership and I signed up for a medical mission to Africa at the end of March. When that was canceled because of COVID-19, I did the next best thing and contracted to work at Elmhurst."

Gloria arrived with our lunch and we took a few minutes fixing coffees and sampling our soups and sandwiches. "So what brings you to Idaho?" I tried for casual.

Those intense eyes studied me for a moment. Rory put her sandwich down and carefully wiped her fingers on her napkin. "Honestly?" She looked me in the eye. "You."

Pleasure rolled over me like a cool breeze on a steamy day. "Me?" Had I really squeaked?

She blushed. "Yes. I," she looked away then brought her gaze back to mine. "I'm in lo…very attracted to you. Since our contracts were ending about the same time, I intended to invite you to spend a couple of weeks with me in Pennsylvania but you got sick before I could ask. At first I thought you were going to die, but when it looked like you were going to make it I hoped you'd let me take you home with me so I could care for you." She shrugged. "But you know what happened. And I didn't have your phone number or address. I finally remembered you'd said you worked at St. Barnabas hospital so I started researching hospitals in Idaho and found this one. I've been offered a temporary job here to deal with the wave of COVID-19 heading this way. But I don't want to assume. Would you be willing to… spend time getting to know each other? Would it be all right with you if I accept the job?"

My smile was so huge I thought my face would split. "Oh, Rory, I feel the same way. I've thought about you constantly since I got home. I tried to contact you but the hospital wouldn't release any information and none of the people we worked with knew so I gave up. I'd love for you to accept the job. I even have an extra bedroom if you want to stay with me while we get to know each other."

Now I wasn't sure which of us had the bigger smile. "I'd love to stay with you."

"One thing I'd like to make clear," Rory said, looking serious. "Once the country gets back to normal I plan to go on that medical mission to provide medical care to displaced children at a refugee camp in Ethiopia. Would you consider coming with me?"

"Wow. That sounds wonderful. Do you think they would want me?"

"I'm positive. And, I'm probably getting ahead of myself and us, but eventually I want to start a low-cost medical clinic in an underserved area, maybe in Idaho, maybe somewhere else." Her eyes met mine again. "With you."

Rory was the woman I wanted, the woman I knew was out there for me, the woman I deserved. I stood, took her face in my hands and kissed her. She responded vigorously. I heard cheering but it took me a minute to realize it was for us. I wasn't even embarrassed. I sat down again and we smiled at each other. "I'll follow you anywhere, Rory."

WORKING AT HOME

J. E. Knowles

It was Day 111 of the pandemic. That's what Tomas said. She dated the pandemic having become a reality in America from the 12th of March, the day the NBA shut down for the season. Raybelle thought of it as the date Tom Hanks and his wife had announced they'd tested positive for coronavirus. That summed up their coping mechanisms anyway: Tomas liked to watch basketball games, while movies were Raybelle's preference.

"Go ahead and watch your movie," Tomas would say, now that basketball was suspended. "I've got work to do."

Always that reminder: Tomas was a doctor, a researcher in virology, while Raybelle was a former senator. With the world on its knees because of a virus, it was if Tomas had been waiting all her life to roll up her sleeves, literally, and get to work. She'd been out of clinical practice for years, but research was going to save the world. Whereas for Raybelle, over sixty and retired, the only safe thing to do was sit in front of the television and wait for the crisis to pass.

Like most people in the world, she was getting tired of waiting.

The longer they lived together, the more Raybelle realized how little they had in common. Of course in a movie, or a romance novel, this always meant the couple was destined for irresistible attraction to one another. And she and Tomas had had that, still did from time to time, but it didn't get them through long summer days and nights and sure as hell wasn't going to get them through COVID-19.

Raybelle was glad Tomas was working. Tomas was glad because she was able to help, to play an active role in addressing the situation. Raybelle was glad for that reason too, but also because it got Tomas out of the house. She worried about her at work, of course she did. But she also knew they'd drive each other crazy, if they had nothing to do but take turns with the remote control.

The fifteen-year age difference had never seemed important before. When things were normal—but Raybelle wouldn't use that word; things hadn't been normal, at least since 2016 when that fool had taken over her party, the Republicans. But if Raybelle had felt increasingly out of place in the Grand Old Party, at least there'd been speaking opportunities; she'd been able to go out and meet people, which is what she'd always liked most about politics. You were supposed to go into public service to help people, as with medicine, and Raybelle had. Her gift as a politician was to be able to walk into a room and just work it. Meeting or re-meeting each person, knowing what to say to him or her.

Now the rooms were off limits, and each person, if she could talk to them at all, was only on the other side of a screen. No handshaking.

Tomas had never been into large events, but she missed the gym. She'd rigged up a pullup bar in one of the doorways and filled the guest bedroom with free weights, for there'd be no guests either. Raybelle had half hoped that these contraptions would end up lying there unused, as so many other people's did. But instead of coming home from work too tired to work out, Tomas found it invigorating. She'd do pullups, set after set of pullups in the doorway; run up and down the stairs, lift dumbbells on the floor upstairs. With every clang of the weights the knickknacks over the fireplace would rattle, and Raybelle would turn up the TV louder. Then Tomas would come in and complain. "You need to get your hearing checked."

"My hearing's fine," Raybelle said.

"Well it won't be, if you keep listening at this volume."

"I'm not making any appointments," Raybelle said, "or going anywhere I don't have to. It's bad enough that you go out."

They hadn't really argued about it until now, June. That was the month when a man named George Floyd was killed by police in Minneapolis, on camera, for the whole world to see. And the whole world was watching, in horror. Raybelle was shocked. She didn't want to watch the video, all eight minutes and forty-six seconds of it, but she couldn't tear her eyes away.

Tomas wasn't shocked.

"What can't you believe?" she said. She was in running gear, stretching for another venture outside, though by this time it was sticky and humid in the Tennessee hills.

"George Floyd," Raybelle said. "Did you know about him?"

Tomas put a hand on Raybelle's shoulder but didn't look at the screen. "I knew about him before it happened."

"We've got to do something about this." Raybelle kept saying that for the rest of the day. "We've got to do something about this."

And Tomas said, "What do you have to do?"

That's when Raybelle looked at her lover, all five foot eight, athletic, still young. And she knew that whatever else Tomas was, handsome and smart and a doctor working to save lives, when people saw her for the first time they registered "black woman." They couldn't help it, Tomas couldn't help it, but she was always going to be black in America. That was something Raybelle could never really understand, but she heard something in Tomas's voice, when she asked, "What do *you* have to do?"

"There's a demonstration," she said a couple days later. "Black Lives Matter. I ought to be there."

Tomas looked askance at her. "Why do you have to be there?"

"Everybody ought to be there," Raybelle said.

"I don't think so."

"Why?" Raybelle waved her hands expansively. "Look, maybe it's been a while, but people in this state respected me. They're conservative, but that meant something then. It did—does not mean, obviously, that black lives don't matter."

"So you have to go as a Republican."

"A retired Republican," Raybelle grumbled. "This shouldn't be a conservative or a liberal issue. I had black voters when I ran, too. There are black conservatives. Nobody should look at that—nobody should be able to watch those videos and say, that's just part of America."

"But it *is*," Tomas said. "When I go out running here, you know what I see? Trump flags. Not campaign signs; flags. Like Trump is America. Do you know how I feel with a mask on? Why do you think I'd rather jump rope in the backyard? And they all have goddamn guns."

Raybelle refused to say the president's name. "You know I would've voted to convict that motherfucker," she said. But Tomas was not impressed with her choice of words.

"It's not just him," she said. "He didn't invent this. He's just exploiting it. Police aren't even the source of the problem—they're enforcing what society tells them to enforce. Black people's lives were in danger a long time before Trump."

"I don't see why the future has to be the same as the past." Raybelle turned back to the laptop. Tomas made fun of her for not using her phone to look up things, but it was all Raybelle could do to let go of her rotary dial.

"I still don't think you should go to a demonstration," Tomas said.

"Why not?"

"It'll be crowded. A big bunch of people together, right in the middle of a pandemic. Trust me, people are still getting sick."

So they argued. Before Raybelle went to the protest, which turned into a string of protests, and when she came home. Tomas worried that her older lover was endangering herself needlessly. "But this is important," Raybelle said.

Tomas stared at her. "I know it's important. I'm a black life!"

"So you understand. It matters!"

"Nobody should be gathering in crowds right now," Tomas said, "believe me. There are black lives being lost to COVID. Disproportionately so. If you worked in medicine—"

"And if you worked where I worked," Raybelle said, "in the Senate. You'd know why I have to be there."

"It sends the wrong message. It says that whether you get together with other people, don't socially distance, depends on how much you believe in the cause. That politicizes it. But the virus isn't political."

"We wear masks!"

"Masks aren't a substitute for not being with other people. Especially those flimsy masks; people just flip them up and down all the time. Touching them makes it worse than not wearing masks at all."

"So what do you want me to do?" Raybelle said. "Stay home and yell at the TV?"

"Sure. That's what you do all the time anyway." Tomas gathered up her personal protective equipment. "I'm going to work."

At that first demonstration, Raybelle and the rest of the crowd walked to the police department, then took a knee, like football players. Passersby, the ones who apparently thought masks were a hoax, yelled at them. Raybelle heard language that would have made her punch the person, especially if Tomas had been around to hear it, but they were kneeling for eight minutes and forty-six seconds. Plus, she wasn't at all confident about standing up again. And you couldn't ask another person for help; touching was dangerous.

"Kneel to God!" screamed a woman across the street. "Stand for the flag!"

Raybelle wanted to yell back, but you weren't supposed to yell either. Yelling could spread COVID too.

She did, eventually, get up. "Hey," she heard someone say. "That's Raybelle McKeehan."

She gave a practiced wave, as if she were Prince Charles. Two young women behind her. She could see they were both white, but not much else, given their faces were covered by glittery fabric masks.

"Good to see you here, Senator," said the first young woman. Her mask was patterned with the American flag.

Raybelle nodded. Her own mask was plain. God help her, she didn't want this thing to go on long enough to get into personalized masks. This was not a thing to get used to.

"So are you still a Republican?" the other young woman said.

"I'm a patriot."

It wasn't her fault, Raybelle wanted to say, that the party she'd spent her life working for had let itself become this crazy populist mess. She didn't say it, though, because she was learning to listen. Other people were talking now: black people, young people. They spoke poetry from the stage. Raybelle didn't always understand poems, but she listened.

Tomas wasn't home when she got back. Against her better judgment, Raybelle switched on CNN. No wonder Tomas thought all she did was rant at the TV.

"It isn't activism," Tomas had said, when they spent more time at home together. But now Raybelle was trying activism, and Tomas said it was too dangerous.

"Why don't you go on Twitter?" Tomas said more than once. "Just, please, no more in-person demonstrations. It's getting hot out there."

Raybelle raised an incredulous eyebrow. "What's getting hot, Black Lives Matter? What Tweets have you been reading? Are they reporting riots?"

"No," Tomas said. "The coronavirus."

* * *

Raybelle had to ration her intake of news, through the election and beyond. She'd always imagined that the first woman to be elected to national office, president or vice president, would be a conservative, someone like Margaret Thatcher. Or herself. She was surprised how affected she was to see Kamala Harris win on the ticket with Joe Biden.

"Never thought I'd be voting for Joe," she said to Tomas. "I remember the first time he ran for president."

"So do I," Tomas said. "I was in high school."

"I'm going to smack your butt."

Raybelle didn't understand exactly what Tomas was researching, though she suspected Tomas was excited about going to work. If you asked her, she'd say, "Chasing variants." So much of virology was done by scientists working all over the world—Europe, China, the Middle East—that Raybelle was faintly surprised Tomas had to leave the house at all. "The lab is pretty much empty," Tomas said. "We're down to twenty-five percent of people; any closer and we couldn't do social distancing. All the assistants and interns, we've had to let go."

"Don't you wear masks anyway?"

Tomas looked at her patiently, as if she were a particularly obtuse student. "Masks aren't a substitute for keeping apart from people," she said. "Stop fetishizing masks."

"I'm not *fetishizing* them." Like Tomas would even know what her fetish was, if she had one.

"I'm just telling you." Tomas crunched her cornflakes, the only pause Raybelle got in her torrent of knowledge. "Masks have become a shibboleth now; you're 'pro-mask' or 'anti-mask.' You 'believe in science' or you don't. But science is not a belief system. It's like saying you believe in gravity; you don't have to get the concept, it affects everybody."

Raybelle sighed. "I sure am glad I'm not in politics anymore."

Tomas looked at her, chewing. "So am I, for our sake," she said. "Not for the country's sake, though. What kind of shape are we in when all the sane people from one party quit?"

This was something Raybelle had thought too, and she kept chewing on it, long after Tomas had left the breakfast table. She chewed on it as Christmas approached and with it, the tensions of yet another day spent in the house alone. Would Tomas make sweet potato pie? Would they argue about the superiority of pumpkin?

Tomas did bake a sweet potato pie. Before they could eat the pie, she had to show it off to her family, on a Zoom call between courses of Christmas dinner. Raybelle didn't have much family anymore and she didn't mind gathering with Tomas's in person, but on the computer, it just felt like everybody shouting after a while. She tried saying "What?" and they just talked more loudly. Volume wasn't the problem. She felt old and crabby and after the pie she said, "I believe I'll lie down for a while."

Tomas twitched her eyebrow suggestively. "Want company?"

Raybelle tried to think of a way to say she had a headache, without sounding like a cliché.

"Hey," Tomas said, "it's okay."

"Honey, I'm sorry."

"I always have my Christmas Day orgasm," Tomas said breezily. "Whether you participate is entirely up to you."

Raybelle gaped at her. "Romance!"

"Twelve years' worth."

* * *

Normally New Year's Eve was not a holiday Raybelle much looked forward to. There wasn't anything special to do this year, of course, but surely to God the New Year was going to be better than the old one. Just getting rid of the 2020 calendar felt good. She and Tomas drank a toast at midnight and then fell asleep. They were exhausted.

Raybelle was more awake on the fifth of January, when the state of Georgia was having runoff elections to decide control of the Senate. She'd never thought she'd see the day she'd be hoping the Democrats would win. It wasn't as though she'd moved to the left, started using words like *cisgender* and *mansplain*. As she often reminded Tomas, she'd never actually quit the GOP.

One of the Republicans running in Georgia, Kelly Loeffler, was trying to retain her appointed seat by attacking her opponent, a black minister. She claimed to be "more conservative than Attila the Hun."

"What the hell does that mean?" Raybelle said, hitting "refresh" on her laptop again. "Louts aren't 'conservative.' It's not conservative to want to tear everything down."

Tomas shook her head. "And Loeffler part-owns a WNBA team. Do you know what those women think of her? Black and white. How can you work with basketball players and have that kind of attitude?"

Raybelle said, "They only care about winning. So much of your energy goes into just trying to stay in office, you forget what you're there for." She remembered. "If Joe and the Democrats were to pull this off, I hope to hell they know what to do with it."

Tomas was in her jogging clothes, getting ready to jump rope, but she sat down for a moment to continue the conversation. Unheard of. "Do you really think there'll be bipartisanship?" she said. "I mean what would that look like? Biden knows the Republican senators, but that doesn't mean they're prepared to spend more money."

"I don't know that he has to cooperate with Republicans in Congress," Raybelle said. "I think what he'll try to do is get things done that *voters* like, even Republican voters. COVID relief. Elected Republicans talk about not wanting to spend money, but when people are hurting, they want money spent on them. Do you know how popular raising the minimum wage is, with people who voted Republican?"

"Yeah. I watched election night." Tomas smiled. "You were so glued to the TV you probably forgot I was there."

Raybelle frowned at the laptop. "Ninety percent reporting," she said, "and both Republicans ahead."

"It all depends where those votes are from," Tomas said. "If they haven't counted most of Atlanta, we could see the same thing happen. Wave after wave of Democratic ballots."

"No wonder people think the election was rigged."

Tomas scoffed, but Raybelle leaned forward to make her point. "No, listen. Most of these…conspiracy theorists don't have a single friend who voted for Joe Biden. Of course they watched the election turn from red to blue overnight and wondered where all those votes came from."

"Because Trump has been saying elections are rigged since before he *won!*"

"*And* because, for all the people listening to him know, no one around them is a Democrat. And we're just as bad. Do we talk, any longer, to people with different politics? Except each other." Raybelle smiled.

Sure enough, the Georgia special election was called the next day for the Reverend Raphael Warnock, Attila the Hun's opponent. The other runoff was closer, but it looked as if the Democrat was going to pull that one off too. Raybelle had CNN on, muted so she didn't have to hear excerpts from Trump giving his damn speech. She kept refreshing the news on her laptop, as if it would answer her questions faster.

Tomas came in. A sweaty but welcome sight. "Hey, lover," Raybelle said. She could use a distraction. Maybe they could make up for Christmas—

"Are you seeing this?" Tomas waved her phone toward the TV. "A mob marching on the Capitol."

"Yeah, I know. I turned the sound off."

"Turn it back on," Tomas said.

Raybelle un-muted the TV to hear the sound of broken glass. What appeared to be someone's phone camera showed a fire extinguisher being used to smash a window of the Capitol building. "I'm not believing this," she said.

For the next two hours they sat mesmerized, Tomas rigid, with phone in hand. "Where is the National Guard?" she said. "Those policemen are totally overwhelmed."

Raybelle wanted to say that there'd been more officers at the Black Lives Matter protest in her hometown than appeared to be guarding the U.S. Capitol. But she couldn't speak. For years she'd worked in that building, with some of the same people who were there today. They'd been certifying the election, and now they were—what? Running for their lives? It wasn't clear, but it was unbelievable.

It was hours before any reinforcements arrived to restore order on Capitol Hill. Hours before Tomas leaned over, put an arm around Raybelle, and said, "You okay?"

"Yeah," Raybelle said automatically, then snapped her gaze away from the screen. "No. I could've been in that building, Tomas. What if that had been me? What if I were on the phone to you now, not knowing how I was going to escape from those bastards? Bastards!"

"I know."

Tomas hugged her and Raybelle shook, not with tears, but with rage. That was *her* Capitol under attack. It was America's place. What people didn't understand was that politicians were human beings. Even the scummy ones, even those Raybelle couldn't stand. And the media, the press people, hiding out in the basement of the building; they were human beings. People, with families, like her. How had this been allowed to happen, that Americans saw each other, not as human beings, but as monsters?

Tomas went for a shower. Raybelle put some spaghetti on to boil. It was like hundreds of previous nights of the pandemic, but different. Raybelle kept one ear open for the TV, for when Congress would return to the floor. For when the betrayals would stop. For some semblance of democratic normality returning to the capital.

Over the garlic bread Tomas said, "I bet you are glad you're retired now."

Raybelle shook the Parmesan cheese, so long and hard that she couldn't see her meat sauce anymore. "Actually," she said, "I think you're right."

"About what?"

"What hope is there, if every sane and sensible person leaves one party? Think about it. The Republicans didn't have a lot of minority support at the last election, but they got more than they did in 2016. There's nothing that says they have to be a white party, a white nationalist party. If they actually offered something other voters wanted. Not everybody is a liberal or a Democrat."

"Well, right now," Tomas said, "the Republicans are more interested in keeping us from voting than in earning our vote."

"That has to change," Raybelle said.

"How?"

"I don't know. But a majority of Republicans now say they support prohibiting discrimination against LGBT people. If that's the case, anything's possible," Raybelle said. "I'm going back to work."

"Don't forget to do the dishes first," Tomas said.

The characters in this short story first appeared in the novel The Trees in the Field *by J. E. Knowles.* Trees in the Field *is available from Bella Books or your favorite retailer.*

INCONCEIVABLE

Blythe H. Warren

"Is this really appropriate?" I asked and swatted at Mira's phone as another contraction hit me.

Mira rubbed my back gently, trying to offer me some kind of comfort while Gail, entitlement incarnate, completely ignored my request for privacy. My relationship with the devil's mentor had improved some since she became my monster-in-law, but it had definitely not advanced to this level of intimacy.

"I always check in at this time," she huffed, sounding hurt that in between contractions I hadn't mustered up the proper joy for our regularly scheduled conversations.

"Can't we reschedule?" I whined, far from comfortable with her taking such an active role in my labor. "I'm kind of preoccupied at the moment." I looked to Mira to save me.

"This really isn't the best time, Mother."

"I hardly see how there could be a better time. If not for this ridiculous pandemic, I would be in the room with you."

"Thank god for the pandemic," I muttered, astounded that the woman who, five years earlier, couldn't stand the sight of my face was, apparently, now eager for a close up of my lady bits. "I just think maybe we could press pause on this while a human being is trying to claw its way out of my body."

"She doesn't have claws, sweetheart. She barely has fingernails."

"Not the point, Mira." I glared at her, begging her to end my teleconferencing nightmare.

"We'll call you back once the baby's here, Mother." Over Gail's protests, Mira ended the call (and fifty percent of my agony). "She's just excited about the baby."

"Because once it's out of me she can stop being nice." Mira favored me with one of her patented "You're beyond ridiculous" looks, which was cut short by a fresh wave of pain. "How did you talk me into this?"

"The usual way." She winked and almost immediately recognized the inappropriateness of flirting at this moment. Though she wasn't wrong.

I remembered exactly what had led to this entirely surprising turn of events.

Cassie had gone out with friends (back when that was a possibility that we all took for granted), and Mira, following a rewarding day at the gallery, entered the living room where I sat on the couch reading *Scientific American*. She leaned against the doorframe and stared at me long enough to break my concentration (which wasn't that long considering the length of her skirt and my keen awareness that we had the house to ourselves).

"Do you need something?" I set the magazine aside and gave her my full attention.

"I need to ask you something."

"The answer is always yes."

She hit me with a coy look and settled herself on my lap. She smelled amazing (as always) and felt so good there against me, she could have asked me to walk across the country on my hands, and I would have agreed.

"Cassie's going to be heading off to college soon."

"I know." I was torn between step-motherly melancholy and staring at Mira's perfectly pouty bottom lip.

"The house is going to seem so empty without her. Maybe it's the right time to talk about having a baby."

This wasn't the first time the subject of kids had come up since we got married. We'd even asked Cassie how she would feel about having a little brother or sister. Everyone was on board except, it seemed, for Mira's body. She suffered two miscarriages before we all agreed that it was just too heartbreaking to try again. We gave up all talk of babies for a couple of years, but once Cassie started applying for colleges, the B-word began making more regular appearances in our conversations.

"I don't want to see you hurt again." I held her a little tighter, sorry to have reminded her of our loss.

"What if we try it another way?" She turned to face me, her skirt riding up as she straddled my lap, which did little to help me focus on her words.

"Do you mean adoption?"

"I was thinking more that you would carry the baby."

"I'm sorry, what?" Surely, I had misheard her.

"I think you should be the one to have the baby." That got my attention.

"How? Why? What?"

"It's not such a bad idea."

"It's a completely bad idea. It's an outrageous idea."

"Why?"

"Because you're the mom. I'm the fun, semi-responsible spare adult. That's been working perfectly well. Just ask Cassie."

"You're every bit the mother I am. Just ask Cassie." She leaned in for a kiss, and I could tell that she already knew she was going to win this argument. "Just hear me out," she said before she resumed the seduction portion of her debate.

Once she started nuzzling my neck, I knew exactly where this discussion would end—with me agreeing to anything she wanted. But since this was a weightier decision than where to order dinner from, I thought I should at least try to inject some actual talk into our conversation.

"Not that I object to this mode of persuasion, but I need something more than your expert kissing to base my decision on."

"You do want another kid, don't you?" Her hands inched their way beneath my shirt.

"You know I do, but I've never even considered being pregnant."

"I think you should. It's such an indescribably beautiful experience. I want you to have it."

"Okay." I drew the word out, not at all convinced that missing out was a strong enough justification for such a major life change. I mean, I'd also never bungee jumped or tried to sell my organs on the black market, but I was fine going to my grave without either of those experiences.

"Plus, the embryos aren't going anywhere." She added another questionable point to her already dubious argument.

"Except in me, apparently."

When she first got married, Mira convinced her otherwise worthless husband that they should take steps to ensure they could have kids down the road, after she established herself in her career. Of course, Cassie came along and thwarted those plans, but not before they'd frozen a few embryos.

"I know it's a big decision, one that we shouldn't make lightly, but I also don't see the downside to trying."

"Not even if it doesn't work?"

"Why wouldn't it work?"

"I'm older than you."

"Only by a year."

"And I've never been pregnant before or even come anywhere close. I'm so far removed from pregnancy that my uterus is probably shriveled up and full of lint. A completely uninhabitable environment unless you want a dust bunny for a kid. What makes you think this will work for me when it didn't for you?"

"Because you're you." Her dark eyes were filled with love, hope and just a hint of sorrow. "Impossible things work out for you, like this relationship. Ask anyone who knew either of us twenty-five years ago if they thought we would ever be happily married to each other, and they would have laughed. But since you came back into my life, I've never second-guessed being with you. It's always been right. You're right. And you make everything better, so I have to believe you'll make this better too."

Well, how could I argue with that? "You know I'm not magic, right?"

"You are for me," she said and then resumed nuzzling my neck, and in the end (after Mira presented her case both on the couch and in the bedroom), we agreed that we would try once more.

If only that had been the hardest part of this enterprise.

The first complication was the timing—had we known about the impending pandemic, we might have reconsidered our decision. Instead, we forged ahead with Operation Knock Liv Up—with great success. Then, about a month after we celebrated the good news of my pregnancy, Governor Pritzker issued the stay- at-home orders that effectively trapped us inside the house where my fluctuating pregnancy hormones had far too many opportunities to collide with Cassie's newfound (and thankfully infrequent) teen moodiness. Our only real breaks from one another came when I went to work. As the pandemic dragged on, she lost hope that her escape to college in the fall would happen, but since Cassie was still Cassie (in other words, the sweetest kid on the planet), she hid her disappointment well. She did, however, spend a lot more time in her room.

Her mother, on the other hand, never dropped below excitement on the emotional meter. Waiting twelve weeks to tell everyone was agony for her, but the second we cleared that milepost, she wasted no time sharing the news with anyone who would listen. Even the semi-impersonal, virus-imposed nature of our announcement didn't cloud her good mood—until it was time to share the news with her mother.

"Do we really need to tell her?" I asked, trying to delay the unpleasant inevitable. "It's not like there'll be any surprise visits in our near future. She never has to know."

"She's my mother. She deserves to know. And when this pandemic eventually ends, she'll probably notice the extra person living in our house."

"Fine," I relented. "But don't be surprised if she's not overjoyed by this." I rested my hand on my stomach, perhaps to shield the baby from Gail's judgmental eyes.

"I'm fully prepared for this to go badly." Mira smiled nervously and added her hand to the protective weight on my belly before opening her laptop.

"At least you can have a drink afterward," I muttered, already wanting this over with. Despite Mira's naïve hope that her mother wasn't entirely malevolent, I remained unconvinced. No way was Gail Butler, Queen of Intolerance, going to be anything less than offended by the fact that her grandchild was now developing in my lesbian uterus. "All I can do is watch my midsection slowly expand."

"Maybe it won't be that bad," she murmured as Gail's severe face materialized on the computer screen.

Her lips were moving, but as usual, she was muted. Despite my suggestion that a silent Gail would make for a much more palatable virtual visit, Mira went ahead and reminded her to unmute herself just in time for the opening insults.

"You both look tired. Perhaps all the extra togetherness of the lockdown is taking its toll. If it's too stressful for you to stay there, Mira, you and Cassie are welcome to join me here." She sounded almost joyful at the possibility of marital trouble.

"We're fine, Mother. There's no stress, and in fact, we have good reason to be tired." Mira took a deep breath, and I braced myself for a blast of judgmental carping. "Liv is pregnant."

This pronouncement was met with absolute silence, a silence so prolonged that Mira checked to see if Gail had muted herself again. She hadn't.

"Mother? Did you hear what I said?"

Gail's mouth opened and closed a few times without any sound emerging.

"I think we broke her," I muttered.

"Mother?" Mira tried again, to no avail.

Then, apparently thinking that having more information would somehow coax Gail out of her extended silence, Mira shared every detail related to this earth-shattering development, including the seemingly good news that, though I was the one carrying the baby, Mira had supplied the genetic material.

As Mira explained the part about the baby inside me really being hers, the dragon lady's face morphed into something closer to joy than anguish. It was hard to say since I'd never seen it happen before, but I swore I saw her smile. I laid a hand on Mira's arm to try to rein in her rambling, and at long last, Gail finally spoke.

"What wonderful news! Congratulations!" It was like a switch had flipped, and suddenly all the good cheer that Gail had suppressed in her life came tumbling out. Her broad smile was unnerving in its unfamiliarity.

"You're not upset about this?"

"Sweetheart, I'm thrilled."

"Are you sure that's your mother?" I whispered to Mira while Gail animatedly chattered about onesies and diaper services.

"Not entirely," she whispered back, just as dumbfounded as I was.

Though I was cautiously relieved by Gail's unexpected reaction, years of being alternately ignored or reviled by her had left me wildly unprepared for dealing with a supportive Gail Butler. I almost would have preferred her hostility to the weirdly attentive alternative.

At first her intrusions into my pregnancy were minor. She sent Mira several articles (in print and via email) detailing all the risks to pregnant women over forty, and she followed up with recommendations for specialists who would be happy to work with a new mother of "such an advanced age." Then she "requested" weekly chats.

"Since I'm prohibited from accompanying you to the doctor, the least you can do is keep me apprised of my grandchild's development."

Though the least thing I wanted to do was carve out regular Zoom and Gloom sessions with my nemesis, I didn't see a way out of it (at least not one that wouldn't result in something even more invasive as retaliation). I figured I could let Mira and her mother do most of the talking and chime in only as needed, hopeful that would satisfy my personal shaitan.

And then the packages started arriving. At first, they were all addressed to "Baby Butler" (no acknowledgment of my considerable contributions) and filled with not at all ridiculous items like Burberry pajamas, an organic crib mattress (for the custom made crib she'd hired an artisan to craft for us), an Armani pacifier and a sterling silver rattle.

Soon our home was overflowing with every infant luxury imaginable (and some that should have remained unimaginable), all of which would eventually end up on the receiving end of a healthy amount of spit up. When we told her that we were running out of room, she offered to let us live with her and, following our adamant refusal, she tried to buy us a bigger house.

Maybe a month after the housing debate, I came home from work to find a humongous package sitting in the center of our living room. Based on Mira's expression (a combination of curiosity, concern and trepidation) I guessed that her mother had bestowed this mighty gift and that I was its intended recipient.

"Whatever it is, remember that it was done out of love."

"I thought it was from your mother."

"Tolerance?" She kissed me then, a reminder of what truly mattered.

I opened the box to find a collection of bespoke maternity wear, none of which I was ever likely to wear without the threat of violence to inspire me. I unfurled dress after dress, some of them frilly, none of them in any way appealing to me. There were enough dresses to last for the duration of a frilled shark's gestation. Even if I entertained the thought of midday wardrobe changes, I would never conceivably make use of all of this clothing, especially since I had no intention of wearing any of it. They were impractical for work, and the likelihood of me donning a floral muumuu at home (no matter how detailed the stitching) was right up there with the current administration believing in science.

Buried about halfway down the assemblage of useless garments, I found a note from my benefactor explaining that she'd noticed how uncomfortable I seemed during our last chat.

She'd seen me fidgeting and tugging at my ever-tighter clothing and had instantly purchased every maternity outfit available on the free market.

Much as I hated to admit it, Gail's act was rather considerate, so I tried to focus on the kindness behind the act (and the fact that kindness was a concept so totally foreign to Gail that she was bound to miss the mark). And if she could be considerate after all this time (even if it was motivated by the bun in my big gay oven rather than by any genuine fondness for me), I could reciprocate her kindness. Swallowing my pride, I grabbed the least hideous addition to my wardrobe and waddled to the bedroom to change.

Mira, obviously curious, followed me and, to her credit, managed to stifle her laughter at the sight of me in a dress. When we both recovered from the shock, we launched a bonus Zoom time with Gail, and I thanked her—genuinely—for her generosity. She praised the fit of my fabulous floral tent, and it was, without question, the nicest conversation we'd ever had.

Regrettably, she took that as her cue to lavish me with attention. Our Zooms happened more frequently, and her overbearing generosity extended to my job as well. Like her daughter, she had reservations about my usual mode of transportation.

"You're pregnant."

"I had noticed that fact."

"What are you doing on a bicycle?"

"Well, the baby hasn't taken control of my legs yet, so—"

"Mira, talk to her."

"I've tried."

"Your stubbornness is endangering the baby."

"I'll stick to side streets. And I promise I won't ask the baby to pedal until the third trimester."

"Nonsense. I'm buying you a car."

"What? No! I don't need you to buy me a car."

"I'm thinking a Tesla if that helps. I know you have environmental concerns."

Again with the misplaced munificence. "I appreciate your concern, but it's really not necessary. Besides, I'm a terrible driver. The baby would be in greater danger with me behind the wheel."

"Then I'll get you a driver."

"Or," Cassie interrupted the adult squabbling, "Mom could drive Liv to work."

I wondered how much her suggestion was motivated by concern for me versus a need for privacy, even if it only came in twenty-minute increments, but I kept that thought to myself. I sat dumbfounded as Mira and Gail negotiated the terms of my regular commute and the last vestige of my personal autonomy was taken from me.

But not even getting her way (more or less) slowed Gail down. A couple of weeks later, after a long day that included a fetal dance party on my less vital organs and a continued onslaught of Gail's aggressive beneficence, I skipped my nightly check-in with the maternity hall monitor (consequences be damned) and went to bed early. I finally found a comfortable position when Mira lay down behind me. She snuggled close and rested a hand on my belly.

"You missed your call with Mother."

"I'm sure we'll make up for it tomorrow," I whined, already dreading the day to come.

"What's wrong? Are you worrying about the baby?"

"In a manner of speaking."

"Translation?"

"Mira, I love you, and I'm thrilled that you're getting along with your mother." I turned to face her then. "I would do anything for you, but, please, you have to save me from her."

"I know she's a little pushy right now—"

"She's tracking my abdominal circumference."

"She's excited about the baby."

"She records my weight and glucose levels. She called me five minutes into my doctor's appointment for updated data. She wanted to FaceTime during my ultrasound."

"She's focused."

"She's impossible," I whined again, but I knew my complaining would get me nowhere. Not that Mira didn't care that I was suffering, but when it came to Gail getting what Gail wanted, there was simply no deterring her. And, there was no doubt that, unpleasant side effects notwithstanding, Mira appreciated her mother's seismic personality shift.

I felt marginally better after talking to Mira—at least I was no longer suffering in silence—but I'd taken to counting down the days until I was free from the unadulterated attentions of Gail Butler. I knew I was being ridiculous. Even Patsy let me know I was being unreasonable. We connected on Zoom the Saturday following my meltdown with Mira. I was at work, taking my lunchbreak with the Giant Pacific Octopus, while Patsy, apparently, was enjoying a liquid lunch.

"Cheers, Mama!" She hoisted her half-empty glass in the direction of her computer. "Have I mentioned how thrilled I am that you married a photographer? I need every picture. I'm thinking of making a flipbook of your pregnancy."

"I'm glad my condition amuses you," I grumbled and took a bite of my contraband SpaghettiOs.

"You're extra grumpy. I thought motherhood was supposed to be joyful."

"It probably is for anyone who doesn't have to deal with Gail Butler."

"What horrible thing has she done now? Bought you a luxury bassinet?" Patsy laughed and poured herself another beer, since she was drinking for two now.

"She's driving me crazy."

"She's being nice. I thought that's what you wanted."

"She's being too nice. It's overwhelming. Yesterday she asked if it would be too much trouble to start monitoring my fluid intake."

"At least she asked."

"And she's called Roman every week to ensure the aquarium is making accommodations for me. If not for the unsuitable construction timeline, she would have donated funds for a special maternity wing. I can hardly go to the bathroom without Gail asking me about the color of my urine."

"She's excited about the baby."

"That's what Mira said."

"Is that such a bad thing?"

"It would be less bad if she cared about me too."

"Are you actually wanting a relationship with your mother-in-law?"

"Maybe I just want to be acknowledged as something more than human Tupperware."

"I'm sure you'll feel the love at the virtual shower we're throwing. Since we can't gather in person, Gail is having the caterers deliver food to everyone's houses. And she took my suggestion of mini Bundt cakes for dessert. They're pink." Patsy seemed inordinately pleased with this development. I, on the other hand, doubted I'd be allowed to enjoy anything that wasn't leafy green.

"What's the point of a shower when she's already provided everything?"

"The point is to celebrate this momentous and apparently not impossible event. Plus, we get to eat and drink on Gail's dime. She's sparing no expense."

"But we don't need her dimes. We're fine."

"I'm sure you are. But maybe she isn't. Maybe this is her Scrooge moment, and you're trying to take it from her."

"Am I really being that unreasonable?"

"We can blame the pregnancy if you want."

"That's only fair since it's the entire reason I'm dealing with the blitzkrieg of benevolence."

"Listen, no matter what her motivation is, she's not going away anytime soon. You won't know if she's sincere or manipulative until—when's your due date again?"

"You know perfectly well that I'm due on your birthday. This is your present, by the way." I couldn't help smiling at her joy.

"Auntie Patsy is going to have so much fun with her birthday twin! Anyway, I say enjoy the ride until then. You've got another few weeks of Gail's version of pampering you which, while it might not be in sync with your personal esthetic, will still be pretty damn luxurious. Your baby will be the only infant on the planet who spits up on million thread count Egyptian cotton sheets. And if she goes back to treating you like the furniture, you won't be any worse off, and your kid will still have it good."

"So I should prostitute myself to spoil this kid?"

"That kid is going to be spoiled by her grandmother, no matter what. I'm saying you should get something out of it while you can." She punctuated her comment with a drink.

"I guess that makes sense," I said and resigned myself to Gail's aggressive altruism.

Unfortunately for Patsy and her pink mini Bundt cakes, the shower never happened, at least not according to plan. Thanks to the early arrival of little Elizabeth Butler-Cucinelli, instead of an elaborate virtual celebration with friends, we were treated to a more intimate gathering the instant we returned from the hospital. Never a patient woman, Gail had camped out in our living room while I was in labor (according to Cassie, her grandmother slept on the couch, and yes, she did provide photographic evidence).

"This is a surprise, Mother. We didn't expect to see you here."

"You should have. I've been quarantining for a month so that I could hold my grandbaby."

She flung her arms out greedily, but I didn't budge. All I wanted was to sleep for a year, or alternately, to stare at my daughter, searing her plump cheeks and tiny hands and her amazing shock of thick black hair into my memory. I had no desire to hand her over for inspection, but I had no legitimate excuse to prohibit Gail from holding her granddaughter. Reluctantly, I placed this tiny morsel of innocence in Gail's arms and held my breath, waiting for Elizabeth's adverse reaction to the embrace of evil, but instead of crying, she simply yawned and burrowed closer to her grandmother. Until that moment, I didn't believe in angels.

"Mother, meet Elizabeth Gail Butler-Cucinelli."

Gail, who evidently did have a heart, gasped and teared up. "You named her after me?"

"And my mother. I may have been delirious at the time I suggested it."

"Thank you, Liv." She cleared her throat (possibly from the effort of calling me by my first name). "I owe you an apology."

"Just one?" I muttered and caught an elbow to the side from Mira. Fortunately, Gail was too enthralled by our newest family member to notice.

"I've been unfairly harsh toward you. All this time, I've expected the worst from you. I worried that you were out to destroy my family, but you've done the opposite." She smiled at the baby in her arms before looking me in the eye. "I'm truly sorry, Liv. I hope you can forgive me."

I shifted nervously and looked everywhere but at the woman who'd been a constant thorn in my side for half a decade. It was inconceivable that we'd reached this place in our thus-far lackluster relationship, but I certainly wasn't going to be the one who prevented us from moving forward.

Even though I had every reason not to forgive her, she was holding the one reason I had to make amends.

"You're not the only one who was expecting the worst. I'm sorry, too."

She smiled at me then, a smile that reached her eyes, and in a move that completely caught me off guard, she handed Elizabeth to Cassie and hugged me. We'd avoided all physical contact up to that point, but once my stupefaction wore I off, I returned the embrace, wondering the whole time if I was experiencing a vivid hallucination.

"I'd love it if we could start over."

"I'd like that too."

Later that night, after Gail returned to her mansion, Mira and I lay in bed listening to Elizabeth sleep. Mira held me in her arms, and exhaustion was just about to overtake me when she whispered in my ear, "You know, we have a perfect, beautiful baby girl, *and* you and my mother are actually getting along. I think you might have to admit that you really are magic."

"Oh, crap."

The characters in this short story first appeared in the novel Bait and Switch *by Blythe H. Warren.* Bait and Switch *is available from Bella Books or your favorite retailer.*

SOJOURNING THE PANDEMIC

Melissa Price

Charlotte uttered a silent and reverent farewell to the home she had just sold, while watching it disappear from her rearview mirror. The goodbye immediately yielded to good riddance, to the life she had never opted for, in the place she had never wanted to live.

The second-guessing of her notion to set out on a long road trip in the middle of a deadly pandemic had to have been at least fifty second-guesses ago—had to have been one of her worst ideas—or maybe her best. Time would tell. She had finally run out of second-guesses and the time to ponder them. Charlotte accelerated onto the freeway, heading west.

Over the three months since she had resolved to divest herself of her life, Charlotte concluded that second guesses were bourgeois, and by the time the sale was complete she hadn't a clue what the next chapter of her life would bring—only that life would serve it to her during a pandemic of catastrophic proportions, without the safe harbor of a home base to secure her well being.

"Why are you doing this now?" Jamie's voice and question echoed on a continuous loop in her mind for the first sixty miles of open desert. And each time he had asked her the question, she packed yet another seemingly endless pile of belongings, and pondered what had compelled her to think that she, a retired swim coach, could make a film—could find a story and then tell it, instead of watching the depressing images on her TV day in and day out. In a glib moment after one of the thousand times Jamie had questioned her judgment, Charlotte realized that she could never steal second base while her foot was still on first. Although she loathed any sports metaphor that wasn't about swimming, in this instance baseball had her sport beat.

She glanced at the backpack on the passenger seat. She hadn't even had time to unpack all the film equipment she had ordered, let alone begun to learn about how to use it.

It doesn't matter that I don't know how to do this, she thought. *I know that there's a story out there in this pandemic and I need to find it and tell it.* She had no inkling of the story she wanted to tell. "I have seven long hours of driving to work it out before I get to the coast," she said to no one.

A seemingly endless proscenium upon which she painted her movie, the open Arizona desert filled with images as her car hummed at 84 miles per hour toward Newport Beach, California. Night had long since fallen by the time she sucked in her first breath of briny air, and each story she had come up with on the ride sadly met its fate in the litter bag.

The last thing she wanted to do by that time was to unload a car full of belongings, carry them down a steep ramp onto the dock, then lift them one by one onto a boat. She'd gotten soft after all the years she had pulled into her garage with a remote control, beyond which lay her comfortable digs. She parked as she'd been instructed inside the shipyard and called the number of her Airbnb host, Monique.

"I've finally arrived," Charlotte said.

Monique gave her instructions to find the 37-foot Carver boat that she'd rented for the month, and then a quick tutorial of what to do if she blew out the electrical circuits. "If you plug in a blow dryer, turn your space heater off, and I'll see you in the morning to answer whatever questions you have," Monique said.

One by one, Charlotte unloaded a car full of supplies she'd packed to keep her safe while traveling during the pandemic. By the time she had loaded her car for the journey, the only free space left in her trunk was enough for an extra pencil.

The harbor made the night feel colder than it actually was, but the beauty of the lights from across the bay more than compensated for it, bouncing off the water, shimmering toward her on a gentle current. Her canned dinner came from one of several bags in her backseat, and she was grateful for it. While she ate, the boat rocked gently and she watched the footage she had shot on her phone in a seedy area of Phoenix the day before she left there. The mile-long stretch of cars extended farther than her eye could see. Nevertheless, the people inside them waited patiently, inching forward to get a bag of food for Christmas from the St. Vincent Food Bank. And not just old cars in line, but expensive cars that contained families who were of means in another time.

She had never been more grateful while eating the can of soup that she had opened, because unlike the people in those cars, she had been able to purchase it. That first night, Charlotte fell asleep to the boat's gentle rocking; the first time she had ever slept without solid earth beneath her. She had already resolved that in uprooting her life, there would be little solid ground on which to rely for comfort—for safety.

The next morning, Charlotte brewed her coffee and sat on the back deck of the boat watching the morning scullers pass her by as their coxswain called out commands to them.

"Ahoy!" The voice had come from behind her somewhere on the dock. "Charlotte?"

Charlotte stood and moved to the deck's door. "You must be Monique." She smiled behind her three-ply mask.

"Hello." Monique put on a mask and climbed aboard. "I see you figured out the coffee pot."

Charlotte chuckled. "I scoped out that Starbucks on Coast Highway just in case. Can I offer you a cup?"

"That would be great thanks."

Charlotte returned with the coffee while Monique took a seat at the table on the deck and reviewed a list of details that made Charlotte glad she would be there for a month to figure it out. "Is there any chance while I'm staying on the boat to take it for a ride?"

Monique smiled at her. "I'll see what I can do. I'm pretty busy here at the shipyard."

"Of course," Charlotte replied. "I know a ride wasn't included in the rental." Charlotte's mind began to wander as she watched Monique—observed her in the way she had sized up her swimmers at the start of every new season.

Monique continued explaining everything from how to shower on a boat, fill up the water tanks, and the rules of the shipyard. Charlotte listened, but mostly she watched the manner in which Monique's manicured hands expressed every thought, the way they punctuated her meaning, and the way her eyes smiled above her mask.

"Any questions?" asked Monique.

"Sure, but I don't even know what they are yet because I'm still on my first cup of coffee."

Monique laughed. "You have my cell number. I'm hard to reach by phone though, so it's better if you text me."

Charlotte stood from the table and the boat rocked just enough to make her smile at the thought that she could feel it. "Thanks, Monique."

Monique left the boat and Charlotte watched her as she moved along the dock back to the office building on land. Monique struck her as a seasoned woman who had her world in order, the rules memorized, which she then conveyed with certainty. But the question begged, what was this refined woman doing in a shipyard in the most opulent location on the Southern California coast? She was startled from her daydream by the barking-dog-ringtone on her phone.

"You made it safely?" Jamie asked with concern.

"Oh shit. I'm so sorry, Jamie. It took me so long to get aboard with all my junk after the long drive last night that I forgot to call you."

"So, how was your first night? Do you have your sea legs yet?"

"It was great to feel my bed rock even though no one else was in it," she laughed.

"It's been way too long since that's happened for you," he replied.

"Don't remind me. My host, Monique, just left the boat after giving me the tutorial. It's a steep learning curve."

"Well then, now you have two steep learning curves."

"You're not kidding. I'm gathering the camera equipment as we speak, and by the time I finish this pot of coffee, I'd better know enough to start using it."

"You will, babe. I have complete faith in you."

"That makes one of us!"

After the call ended, Charlotte laid all the new gear out on the table and she Googled the use of each item. By afternoon, the camera was attached to the gimbal stabilizer, the anamorphic lens was attached, and the film app talking to the gimbal. She gathered the equipment, put it back in the backpack and set out to drive Coast Highway on her way to her favorite place just down the road, Laguna Beach.

Cars that she couldn't identify passed her and at each red light, she caught up to them to read the names on the back. In her time, a Lamborghini was synonymous with "expensive sports car," but now they evidently manufactured SUVs. It seemed unnatural to her, but then again Newport Beach had built its reputation on unnatural opulence, on things like cars that were only recognizable at a glance to those of extreme wealth who could afford them. By the time the light turned green, she realized that the Ferrari dealership whose showroom display must have totaled over a million dollars, had a "For Sale" sign on the window. Perhaps the McLaren dealer had been luckier since there was no sign of attrition. She accelerated past the Lamborghini SUV and renamed it a "Lambordoodle," since every breed now seemed to be crossbred with a poodle.

Charlotte parked the car and walked along the beach in Laguna. There, she met an older woman walking a Pomeranian. "I'm making a short documentary about the effect the pandemic has had on people. Would you be willing to answer a few questions on camera?" asked Charlotte.

After a hesitant moment, the woman answered, "Sure, why not?"

Charlotte clumsily attached the gimbal to the camera, opened the film program and turned it on. By the time a few minutes had passed, Charlotte had her first interview of a retiree on a fixed income who had had a thirty-year business as a pet sitter. The woman had given up her apartment of twenty-eight years due to the fact that all of the wealthy people for whom she had worked were no longer traveling, thereby causing her pet sitting business to grind to a halt.

After the interview, Charlotte took photos of the multi-million-dollar homes that dotted the cliff. Homes whose gardeners probably earned more than the average working American, once one considered what it took to keep those homes looking as elegant as they did. She waited in Laguna Beach to capture the ocean sunset that she had longed to see every night while living in the desert.

On her way back to the boat, Charlotte glanced at a highly manicured woman in the car next to her at a red light. *What the hell is* that *car?* She let the woman speed ahead of her in order to read the label. "A new Aston Martin? I thought those cars were only in James Bond movies!" In that moment, she realized that all of the Aston Martins and the Lambordoodles competing for attention were not unique at all. Unique, was driving a six-year-old Kia on the Newport Beach coast. Suddenly, she wondered how many of the families in the food line in Phoenix could be fed for the cost of *one* Aston Martin. So far, it seemed to her that the people who could afford those cars had no awareness of anything but how shiny their car looked driving along Coast Highway. She stopped at a sandwich shop and brought her dinner back to the boat.

While reviewing her footage of her beach interview, she tried to ignore the fact that for almost a year she had navigated and weathered the pandemic alone, envious of her partnered friends who'd had someone with whom to share this awful experience, and the gift of seeing and being close to another human. The closest she had gotten to that was saying goodbye to Jamie at a six-foot distance behind masks, without even the hug of her best friend as a send-off. But she was good at being alone! Wasn't she? Isn't that what had defined her life for the past five years? Wasn't she the woman who had said to her friends, "I'm done with relationships."

Her text message alert dinged. It was Monique messaging that she had a break in her schedule the following day, and wanted to know if Charlotte was interested in taking a ride on the Carver. Charlotte answered immediately with a "Yes" followed by what must have been fifty exclamation points. Monique texted back with an "LOL" and set the time for the next morning.

Promptly at 8 a.m., Monique arrived on the dock and asked if Charlotte had ever been to Catalina Island.

"No," Charlotte replied, "but I've always wanted to go there."

With the expertise of a veritable sailor, Monique climbed aboard and attended to the rigors of a for-real captain. As they motored slowly out of the harbor, they passed a large buoy on whose surface slept layers of sea lions.

"Before we head out to sea, Monique, would you make a circle around the buoy so I can get closer to the sea lions? I've never seen one up close."

Monique gently turned the boat and Charlotte grabbed the camera, set it to video, and called out to the pile of sea lions basking in the sun. They responded to her voice, barking and looking directly at her.

"They like you, Charlotte!"

"Wow, Monique, that alone made the trip worth it."

Monique laughed and accelerated out into the open ocean. They said little for the next hour as Charlotte's body synched to the movement of the boat in the waves, breathing in deeply as the wind sprayed the bow—exhaling the isolation of nearly a year indoors. The air had never smelled fresher to her. Her line of sight followed Monique's finger as she pointed to a pod of dolphins swimming toward them. With unexpressed childlike excitement, Charlotte thought that for a moment she had won the lottery. Her eyes followed the dolphins' path and for an instant she caught their laughing chatter as they swam close and then performed tricks around the boat before swimming away.

Shortly before they would have reached the dock in Avalon on Catalina, the boat's engine sputtered and then cut off. "Dammit! I'll bet it's that fuel switch I paid good money to have fixed before you arrived!" Monique said.

"What do we do?" Charlotte asked with alarm.

Monique looked at her and hesitated before answering. "The easiest way to reach the switch is from the water, but I'm not a swimmer. I guess I'll have to radio for a tow boat to come get us."

"Wait," said Charlotte as Monique held the radio mic in her hand. "Is there any way you can talk me through it? I'm a swim coach and other than the fact that the Pacific is notoriously cold, as long as I'm not in for longer than a few minutes, I can do it."

"I think we should just get a tow and handle it on Catalina."

Charlotte smiled. "I suppose we have a different senses of adventure. Come on, let's at least give it a shot before you call."

Monique thought for a moment before answering. She reached under her seat at the helm and handed Charlotte a life vest. "Okay," she said warily, "but when I tell you to get back on board, no arguments."

"Deal," Charlotte replied. She latched the life vest around her and jumped overboard.

Monique talked her through the reset of the switch from the deck, but as she reached for Charlotte's hand to pull her back on board, she lost her footing and fell overboard.

"Oh no! Help!" screamed Monique as she floundered in the wave.

Charlotte wrapped her arms tightly around the woman and held her close. "Look at me!" she commanded. As soon as Monique complied, Charlotte's voice became calm. "Don't fight, Monique. I've got you." She felt Monique's body yield before she pushed her upward, Monique grabbing the ladder for dear life and then climbing back on board.

The engine of the "Absolute Freedom" turned over on the first try.

"Damn, girl, you did it! I'm impressed!" said Monique. She paused. "Thank you for rescuing me. But to be sure we're seaworthy, I'm going to radio ahead and get someone from the shipyard to have a mechanic waiting for us."

"That's a good plan." Charlotte went below and returned with two dry sweatshirts and turned her back to Monique to change. She finally had the notion that maybe this 'sojourning the pandemic' hadn't been such a bad idea after all. Only two days in and she was already having the adventure of a lifetime.

When Monique ended her radio call, she looked at Charlotte. "We have a slight problem."

"Oh?"

"The mechanic can't see us until late afternoon, and by then it'll be too late to head back to Newport so it looks like we'll have to spend the night aboard."

"Okay. Well that shouldn't be a problem, should it?"

"No. We have two bedrooms and two bathrooms, so if you're comfortable with that..."

"Why wouldn't I be?"

Monique's face relaxed. "Great."

After spending the late afternoon exploring Catalina Island, the women picked up some takeout and brought it back to the boat in time to capture the spectacular sunset.

Charlotte sighed. "I've never seen a sunset that can compare to this one." She glanced at Monique. "You look sad."

Monique shrugged. "That's what my ex used to say—about the sunset, that is. We used to bring the boat here a lot."

Charlotte raised her eyebrows. "You're gay?"

"Yes," Monique answered.

"Me too."

In that moment their gaze lasted a little longer than it might have, and suddenly the sea spray was filled with wonder, or maybe it was possibility. By the time sleep was imminent, they had both relaxed enough to share their backgrounds and how they had dealt with the isolation of being single women in a world where their possibilities for a future had been stymied.

At about three a.m., Charlotte awoke to the rocking of her bed on the ocean, to the sweet smell of brine, and the chill of the night on the water. She threw a coat over her sweats and climbed to the back deck to gaze up at the stars, to breathe in her newfound freedom. In that moment, she realized that this was the first time in her life she felt truly free. Free of schedules, free of obligations, free of the stories she had been trying for years to leave behind. The boat rocked gently and the breeze howled through the canvas.

"Couldn't sleep?" Monique said softly from behind.

Charlotte gazed into her eyes and smiled with genuine warmth. "It's more like I didn't want to miss this moment."

"Mind if I join you?" asked Monique.

"I'd love that." She paused. "Perhaps this will become a moment that someday neither of us will have wished we missed."

Monique stepped toward her and stopped a few inches away. "You think so?"

Charlotte took her hand. "I really think so," she said softly.

Monique stared into her eyes, closed the space between them and kissed her.

"Great kiss, Monique. And definitely unexpected."

"Well," Monique began, "I wanted to do that just in case you're right about looking back in the future."

Charlotte remained silent for a moment. "Well, in the event that we get to look back at it together, how about we make this even more memorable?"

Monique smiled shyly, took Charlotte's hand and led her below deck.

SEX, LIES, AND BILLOWING CAPES

TJ O'Shea

It wasn't like they never lied to each other. Over the past six years white lies made an appearance as often as severe weather—once or twice a year, never lingering and not memorable. Subtle, harmless little fibs. A lie about a gift so its contents would remain a secret. Lies about how many drinks were consumed at the bar—one or two less than actually imbibed. White lies, half-truths, omissions, and truth-adjacent phrases, all of these were something Iris felt fell well within the parameters of a healthy relationship. She was certain these were allowable offenses.

When the city went into lockdown and stay-at-home orders were issued, Iris laughed at how her straight friends lamented the now constant contact with their partners. Facets of their lives they withheld from each other would now see the light of day, like ants under the floorboards, emerging one by one. Pests that must be dealt with, lest they overrun a happy home.

Iris laughed because she and Sophie did not have those worries. They got along, so famously in fact it was how they got close. They gravitated toward one another during group hangouts, often eschewing their friends in favor of being alone together. Even from the beginning, Iris was covetous when it came to Sophie, because everyone loved Sophie. She was the pillar of their friend group—gorgeous, smiling, quick with a joke, and the first person to volunteer to help any friend in need. Sophie was someone everyone wanted to be around. Her confidence put others at ease, and it was a confidence she projected as easily as the sun creates light. Iris, however, was none of those things. She was quiet, withdrawn, the friend who smiled politely at jokes but was much better at listening than talking. Iris was the friend with a comfortable couch and decent wine, who could talk you through a breakup or emotional rift. So, when Sophie took an interest in her, Iris held on for dear life. To be loved by Sophie was like standing directly under a spotlight, illuminated and warm, while everything else was dark. Iris, in turn, was steadfast and loyal. She got to see the other sides of Sophie she never showed their friends—the bits of trauma, the insecurities—and their transition from friends to lovers was easy and fulfilling, like the growth a flower from a seed.

If Iris were forced to pick a bugaboo about Sophie, her wonderful, lovely Sophie, it would be that Sophie was away a lot. An amateur filmmaker, she would frequently take day trips, overnight trips, weekend trips, sometimes stretches of weeks or months where she would disappear, deep in a remote location to film bonobo monkeys or sitting on top of a skyscraper filming a daredevil tightrope-walking between buildings. Some of these projects would later surface at indie festivals, others Iris never saw at all.

Their friends were more insecure about it than Iris. "Are you sure she isn't cheating?" they'd ask. "Oh, sure, a 'business trip,'" they'd say, elbow-nudging and full of insinuation. More plainly jealous friends outright claimed Sophie had another life on the other side of the country. Iris laughed politely, as was her way, but she never found it funny. Not because she was suspicious, but because she worried for Sophie when she was away. Upon her return she'd be sporting a new bruise, have a harrowing story to tell, or omit days of her trip entirely and Iris was left to imagine what kinds of adrenaline-fueled nonsense she'd gotten up to. And, most importantly, she missed her. So, it was not her favorite thing in the world that her girlfriend was an artist committed to a life of chasing danger, but she supported her and trusted her, and that was that.

Selfishly, Iris was inwardly thrilled about their stay-at-home orders because it meant Sophie could not take off at a moment's notice. Her bag remained unpacked, her cameras tucked away, and while the world grappled with loss and change, Iris secretly reveled in the continued, uninterrupted proximity to her girlfriend. They enjoyed late breakfasts, prolonged bedroom snuggles, an increased frequency in intimacy, and the wonderfully bonding experience of baking bread. A domesticity they'd never had before, that Iris didn't know she craved.

Then, of course, Sophie found a way to leave. Once the strict orders were lifted, Sophie grabbed her camera and her bag, put on a facemask, and took to the streets to film the changes in their neighborhood. Iris couldn't help but feel disconsolate. Her job, boring old marketing, kept her homebound without any reason to go chasing Sophie into action. So, while Sophie was gone less, she was gone more than anyone really should be during a pandemic.

But Sophie never seemed scared. Not for herself, at least. Though that was part of Sophie's allure—her breathtaking bravery. Iris found it strange Sophie possessed no fright of the virus. Not out of disbelief—they watched together as the numbers climbed and Sophie held her a little tighter each time—but perhaps false bravado based upon past lack of illness. Sophie was never sick. Not a cold, not flu, barely even a cough. No matter where she ventured, and she went to plenty of disease-ridden backwaters, Sophie returned unscathed. A strong constitution, she said. Hereditary resistance against infectious diseases, she said. Not that Iris really grilled her on it, but it lingered in the back of her mind as Iris caught seasonal sniffles and Sophie remained blissfully unaffected.

And now, staring at the television screen, Iris felt like an absolute idiot for not seeing it sooner.

There was Sophie—clad in an orange eye mask (and face mask), gradient orange spandex costume, and billowing purple cape—shouldering a helicopter on her back. Sophie was as unmistakable as the sun in the sky. Her gorgeous green eyes, her flowing strawberry-blond hair, the shape of her that Iris knew inside and out. Sophie in flight, carrying an actual helicopter, and then placing it gently on the ground. People clapped, first responders breathed a sigh of relief, and police surrounded the area and kept it clear of media. Except this person and their iPhone, who must have sold it to the local news station, the same local news station Iris tuned in to out of habit. Normally they avoided televised news—they got their news online like normal Millenials—but the pandemic made them obsessively check their local news for updates on virus cases and the government's response.

And where typically Iris would see a woman in a facemask relaying a grim report at a desk six-feet from an infectious disease expert, she instead saw her girlfriend defying gravity and saving a helicopter full of firefighters.

Her girlfriend was superhuman hero Captain Starlight.

Pausing the report, Iris took a breath and washed the dishes. She fed the cat. She sat on their balcony as the sun receded into the horizon and dipped below the skyline they called home. She made tea.

And Iris waited. Iris was good at waiting. Loving Sophie meant being very good at waiting.

Sitting at their kitchen table, Iris looked up as the front door opened and closed. Chloe, their gray-and-black shorthaired cat, slinked along toward the noise and meowed at Sophie's incoming figure. "Chloe-kitty," Sophie cooed at her, reaching down to scratch her chin. "What a good girl."

Sophie took off her facemask and put her bag on the floor in the hallway, rolling her shoulders as she entered their kitchen. Immediately, she stopped in her tracks. Iris blinked at her. "Good day?"

Maybe intuition was one of her superpowers, because Sophie hesitantly nodded and took only one step into the room. "Yes? Is…everything okay, babe?"

"I don't know, *babe*, is everything okay?"

"I'm okay. You seem…upset?"

Iris clenched her hands around her mug of tea. "Do I? Do I seem *upset*?"

Sophie furrowed her brow and crossed her arms over her chest. "You're answering all of my questions with questions, so I'll go with yes, you're upset. Did something happen? Is everyone okay? Your parents?"

Stupid, kind Sophie with her concern for Iris's elderly parents. It nearly disarmed her, but then she remembered the sight of Sophie holding up an entire helicopter and her anger was renewed. "My parents are fine. Everyone is fine. Before I show you something, I want to ask you a question. I want you to stop and think before you answer me, okay?" Sophie nodded. "Is there anything you'd like to tell me? Anything at all?"

As if anticipating an ambush, Sophie carefully looked around the room. It was an ambush, in a way, but there was no enemy hiding behind their mid-century sofa. Just Iris, Chloe, and the elephant in the room so enormous Iris was surprised any of them fit inside the apartment at all. "I—I don't think so?"

"Okay." Iris stood up, calmly strode to the television and turned it on. In a blink Sophie appeared in the middle of the screen in all her orange spandex-clad glory. Arms crossed, Iris did what she was best at: she waited.

"Oh. Oh crud."

Scoffing loudly, Iris tilted her head. "'Oh crud?' 'Oh *crud*?'" she repeated, louder the second time. "At what point were you planning on telling me you were a superhuman with superpowers, Sophie? Because I feel like six years in, Sophie, there must've been an opportune moment. Like, literally any moment. You could've picked any moment in the last six years, Sophie."

"You're saying my name a lot and it's very scary."

"Am I? Am I saying your name a lot, Sophie? Is that even your name? Is that a cover?" Iris looked stricken. "I am going to be *extremely* displeased with you if I find out the name I call out during sex isn't your real name."

Head bowed, Sophie toed the carpet with her boot. "It's my real name."

"Good, great, good." Iris paced the floor, watched carefully by Chloe, who jumped on the table to get a better view of the action. With a groan, Iris ran her fingers through her hair. "All right, okay, let's get down to brass tacks: what the actual fuck?"

"I think you should sit down, babe," Sophie replied, gesturing to their kitchen table. Petulantly, Iris plopped into the seat and kept her arms crossed. Chin out, she waited defiantly for what should be an extraordinary explanation. "Let me start first by apologizing."

"I will consider your apology at a later time."

"Fair enough." Exhaling slowly through her mouth, Sophie straightened her shirt and cleared her throat. "I won't waste time explaining to you the ins and outs of my powers, because I don't think that's important to you. As a quick recap, I can fly, run at super speed, I have the strength of dozens of humans, and I'm fairly impervious to harm. I have been this way my whole life." Iris nodded, recalling the time a chef's knife slipped in Sophie's hand, but she refused to let Iris tend to her. By the time Iris got to look at her hand, it was devoid of any wounds. "Obviously, the main point is I hid this from you."

"Yes, I believe that is the bigger issue here," Iris replied primly.

"It isn't because I don't trust you, I don't want you thinking that. I trust you more than anyone else on the planet," she said, her tone soft and heartfelt. "The League—that's the organization all the superhumans belong to—is crazy about privacy. That's why they insist we wear those ridiculous costumes and disguise our identity."

Iris snorted. "Not very well."

"Right, typically we don't work within a certain radius of our homes for that reason. I was on my way back from something else when I saw the helicopter going down. Typically Red Heart would've been on the case, but she was busy. We're all a little busier these days."

Red Heart was a sultry siren of a superhuman, with a blood-red costume and full red-feathered headdress, who often showed up at crises in their city. Their friend circle was obsessed with her—most people were obsessed with their local superhumans.

Fawned upon like celebrities; their public lives were excessively examined and their mysterious private lives kept the people salivating for more. Iris's interest was extremely casual. Well, until now. Now her interest had gone from 'something I scrolled past on CNN' to 'intimately involved with for the last six years.'

"So, you and all the superhumans, you're friends?"

Sophie shrugged. "For the most part. I only see them once a year at the League Conference and we try not to fraternize too much. Having all the superhumans in one place is a recipe for disaster."

"One can imagine."

Licking her lips, Sophie elaborated, "So, we are forbidden from telling anyone about our identities, including significant others."

"And your parents?" Iris inquired, picturing the affable Mr. and Mrs. Cordell with their big smiles and welcoming arms. It was hard to imagine one of them hoisting a helicopter onto their back. Mrs. Cordell did cross-stitch. Mr. Cordell was a terrible bass fisherman. Were they superhumans, too? Had Sophie's adorable older parents also lied directly to her face? At Thanksgiving? On *Christmas*? "Do they know?"

Nodding, Sophie tucked her lip between her teeth. Iris stared at Sophie's mouth, imagining the way she would bite it as they kissed, but no matter what she did she never drew blood. Not that she was trying to hurt Sophie, but it had struck Iris as odd. All of these quirks, all of these random integers that Iris never considered adding up, all of them pointed to the same truth. "Yes. They are the only ones who know. My parents are not superhuman, but someone else in my family is. That's how it works for most of us. We inherit it from somewhere: parents, uncles, aunts, or grandparents, whatever. There doesn't seem to be a rhyme or reason to it, and the League forbids us from doing DNA tests to determine how it is disseminated into the population."

Silent but thoughtful, Iris bobbed her head, staring down at the table. She reached forward and stroked Chloe's fur, eliciting a purr from their feline. Chloe hopped down and skittered away, and Sophie took the seat opposite her at the kitchen table. "I'm sorry I couldn't tell you. And I'm sorry you found out from the news."

"That's this pandemic's fault," Iris replied with a shrug. "I wouldn't watch the news if it wasn't like, life or death that I do so. I probably never would've found out."

Sophie paused, peering at her boots in introspection. "Probably not. Do you—do you have any questions for me?"

Multitudes, but Iris evenly considered all of them before replying. "Do you actually make those films, or is that just a cover?"

Brightening a little, Sophie smiled. "No, those are real. I use my deployments—that's what we call getting called out to a crime or an event—to make my films. Those are very real. It's important to me and most superhumans that we are allowed to have lives outside the rescue stuff."

"Mhm." Iris clasped her hands in front of her. "What did you do on Christmas two years ago? I thought when you said there was an 'emergency' you were lying to get out of having to see my sister."

"I was evacuating civilians from a sandstorm near the UAE," Sophie replied. "Not having to sit through another one of your sister's tedious parties was an unexpected bonus."

"They are so bad," Iris commiserated. "It is exponentially worse without you there."

Sophie frowned. "I know, I'm sorry."

Another thought popped into Iris's head. "Why do you wear a facemask? Aren't you…unable to catch viruses?"

"Yeah, our immune systems are insane, but it's about the optics. Gotta be a good role model for the kiddies. And the adult…ies."

Iris smiled softly, because of course Sophie would do her part as an upstanding citizen. "When you say impervious to harm, how impervious are we talking? You've come home really beaten up before."

Scratching the back of her neck, Sophie shrugged. "It's hard to tell. Nothing a typical human can do to me would hurt me. One time I got caught in a hurricane and it picked me up for like a mile and then smashed me into a barn. That bruised a bit."

"If you're that strong, how did you get a black eye that one time?"

Sophie snickered. "Hiro accidentally socked me. We were deployed to Australia during the wildfires and it got hazy in the smoke. It wasn't his fault. Kangaroos get real punchy."

A long silence fell between them. Six years of trust and commitment hung in the balance of this reveal. And Iris couldn't go anywhere to work through it. Maybe take a walk in the park, but she couldn't meet with a friend, or even stare longingly out of a coffee shop window. No, she was stuck here, inside, with her treacherous superhuman girlfriend. Her treacherous, superhuman girlfriend who looked, maybe for the first time, worried and anxious. Perhaps it should've made Iris feel powerful to be in control, but it didn't. There was only frustration and hurt.

"How are you feeling?"

Rolling her eyes, Iris sat back against her chair and shrugged. "I feel like Sally Field in *Mrs. Doubtfire*. That's how I feel, Sophie. I just want to shout 'the whole time?' at you, over and over again. Like, remember how obvious it was that Robin Williams was Mrs. Doubtfire? Like he barely looked different, he almost blew it so many times, but somehow Sally Field just doesn't see it. His own kids don't see it! I feel like Sally Field and Matilda, and…his other two children. I feel duped, and stupid."

Wincing, Sophie reached across the table and tried to take Iris's hand, but she snatched it away and plunked it in her lap. "You're not stupid. The whole point of keeping my superhuman identity a secret is to protect you. You are never supposed to find out, because if you did, someone could try to hurt you to get to me. For what it's worth, I hated lying to you. None of the deception they insist upon brought me any joy."

Sure, the words coming out of Sophie's mouth sounded reasonable, but Iris didn't want to hear them. She felt foolish. The years she spent adoring this woman and she barely knew her. All the late nights waiting up for her, thinking she could get kidnapped and held for ransom by a group of bandits on a Peruvian mountain pass. Only to find out Sophie could throw those men off a mountain without even breaking a sweat.

Softly, Iris whispered, "Why are you with me?"

Eyes wide, Sophie scraped the chair against the floor and got close enough for their knees to touch. "What are you talking about? What do you mean 'why?'"

"Sophie, come on. Look at you. You're beautiful and smart, and you're so funny and charismatic. People fall over themselves just to be in your presence, and they don't even know the half of it, do they? They don't know that on top of being an amazing person, you're an amazing super-person." Shaking her head, Iris exhaled a trembling sigh. "And me? I'm not as smart, or socially conscious, or as friendly as you are. But somehow, I get to be close to you, to love you, to support you, and I'm grateful that you choose to be with me."

"It's not a choice," Sophie replied in a small voice.

Still in her own head, Iris continued. "Now I don't understand why you'd ever want to be with me. I'm not exciting, I'm not adventurous. God, the incredible things you must see on a daily basis and then you come home to me, and I'm like, 'Oh hey Sophie, come look at this crossword puzzle with me because I'm too dumb to come up with a seven letter river on the African continent,'" Iris bemoaned, rubbing her forehead. Tears filled her eyes, threatening to spill over. "God, I'm so boring. All these weeks stuck inside with me; you were probably aching to get out of here. This pandemic must be the worst thing ever for you. Not able to see the world, or rescue people, or have fun punching tornadoes with your super-friends. No, you're stuck sitting in this dumb apartment with me and the cat, watching our sourdough starter rise."

Pushing her chair with the back of her knees, Sophie stood and crossed her arms, peering down at Iris. She possessed an aura of authority Iris admired. Their friends called it her 'mom energy' but Iris felt it was something deeper. Something more intrinsic to who Sophie was—she was simply built to be in charge. "Are you done?"

Iris nodded, sniffling. "I guess."

Taking a knee in front of her, Sophie placed both her hands on Iris's lap. "Baby, I love you, but everything you just said is such hot garbage I wish one of my superpowers was to scrub it from my brain."

"Well, that's a little harsh."

"Yeah, I know, but I have to be harsh because I've never heard you say that much bullshit in one go in the past six years. That includes the time you tried to convince me the Backstreet Boys were better than NSYNC."

"They're the best-selling boy band of all time."

"Yet despite having more albums than NSYNC, they have the same amount of top ten hits, so," Sophie replied with a dismissive shrug. "But this is not about that. This is about you and all that crap you just spewed about yourself. None of that is true."

"Oh, I didn't realize truth-detecting was one of your superpowers," Iris mocked glumly.

"It isn't, but it could be where you're concerned." Holding her hands tightly, Sophie inhaled a deep breath and implored her. "Iris, being with you isn't a choice. I didn't just pick you out of a hat and decide to spend my life with you. I fell in love with you completely out of the blue. You've totally bewitched me, do you understand?"

Iris shook her head. "That's not possible."

"I don't think you get to tell me what's possible," Sophie replied in a stern voice. "I literally carried a helicopter today. That shouldn't be possible. But it is. I can toss eighteen-wheelers into the sky and I am in love with you, Iris Lowe. Both of those things are possible. Both of those things are true."

Wiping tears from her cheek with her shoulder, Iris took in Sophie's earnest expression and large, intense eyes. "You have to know how hard it is to believe that."

"Why?" Sophie pressed. Iris didn't respond, so Sophie dug into her pocket and withdrew her phone. Tapping on it with her thumb, she turned it around and showed Iris a photo. "See this? This is my costume from ten years ago."

"Look how short your hair was," Iris replied in a whisper, smiling. "But, so what? It looks like the one I saw."

"No, it doesn't." Sophie flipped the phone back to face her and swiped through photos, landing on a newer one. "See? Now the cape is purple. The cape used to be a darker orange."

"And?"

Making a frustrated noise in the back of her throat, Sophie shook the phone at her. "It's purple for you, *Iris*. Purple like an *iris flower*. I made them incorporate it into my costume a few years ago. I wanted…I wanted a little bit of you with me when you can't be there. I wanted the reminder that part of the reason I do what I do is because it keeps the world safe for you."

Iris wanted to scoff. She wanted to scoff, but she knew Sophie was being genuine—because Sophie was always genuine. The great irony of this reveal was Sophie didn't possess a disingenuous bone in her body, so the fact she managed to keep up a charade for this long was almost admirable. And Iris knew what Sophie said was true, and of course she was touched and charmed by it. "Oh. Should you have those photos on your phone?"

"Trust me, this phone is more secure than the Pentagon."

"Well, that makes me feel better for you. A little worse about the Pentagon."

Putting her phone away, Sophie kneeled completely in front of Iris and took both her hands again. "So, sure, I have seen a lot of the world and tons of cool stuff. However, the fact remains, Iris, you fascinate me more than any world wonder ever could. No matter where I go, the place I want to be most is anywhere you are." Swallowing, Sophie lowered her gaze to Iris's lap. "Listen, if you need space I'm willing to get out of your hair for a bit. I understand this is a lot to process."

"No," Iris quickly interrupted. Sophie's round, hopeful eyes peered up at her. "No, I don't—I don't like when you're away. Don't leave."

"Okay," she said. "I'll do whatever you need me to do."

Iris fell silent once more. Detaching her hand from Sophie's, she reached forward to run it through the gentle curls of her hair. Sophie leaned into the touch, eyes fluttering closed. "Will The League be angry I know about everything?"

"Angry? No," Sophie murmured, holding Iris's hand against her cheek. "No doubt the video you saw has been scrubbed and honestly, I don't think anyone else would've recognized me as quickly as you did. But I will have to tell them that you know."

Fear crept into Iris's brain. "What will they do?"

"I don't know. Probably make you sign an NDA or something."

Sighing in relief, Iris stroked Sophie's cheekbone with her thumb. "Oh. I thought they were gonna like…put a bag over my head and recondition me in an undisclosed location. Or worse: make you break up with me."

"Please," Sophie replied with a sneer. "If it's a choice between you or them, there's no question. It's you, always."

And there it was, Sophie's confidence, directed at Iris and no one else. The spotlight keeping her warm. Iris lifted her other hand to cup Sophie's face and bring them close, kissing her softly. "Beguiling sweet talker."

Sophie's lips widened in a grin against her own. "Am I forgiven?"

"Getting there," Iris replied, kissing her once more before pulling away. "No more secrets, okay? I understand if you have to keep state secrets or world-saving kind, but at least keep me informed enough to know you're okay. Promise?"

"I promise," Sophie said immediately.

"Good. Now, I am requesting to be picked up bridal-style and carried into our bedroom where you can continue to make it up to me." Iris held out her arms. "Let's go, Captain. Get to work."

Giggling, Sophie stood up and swept Iris into her arms as if she weighed nothing. Iris blushed, wrapping her arms around Sophie's neck. She leaned up and pressed their lips together, more wantonly than before. Sophie smiled as they broke apart. "Anything you want, my darling."

She strode toward their bedroom, until Iris shot out her hand and grabbed the doorjamb. Sophie halted, eyebrow raised. "Wait. This means when we moved in together you could've carried everything up here yourself and not broken a sweat?"

Sophie bit her lip and nodded. "Yes. But that would've blown my cover, babe."

"Forget your cover! I was sore for days!" Iris's mouth fell open. "You made me help you carry the couch up several flights of stairs. You could've just, I don't know, floated it up here!"

Throwing her head back in laughter, Sophie carried her into the bedroom and gently laid Iris on the bed. Straddling her waist, Sophie went to lean in but Iris sat straight up into her space. Sophie rolled her eyes. "Yes?"

"You gave me such crap about how many books I moved into this apartment," Iris recalled, poking Sophie in the sternum. "'Iris, this is way too many books. The boxes are too heavy.' Meanwhile you could've juggled ten boxes of my books!" Iris gasped. "You just didn't want me to bring all my books here. Deceits upon deceits."

Fondly gazing down at her, Sophie shook her head. "I love you very much, Iris darling, but you are a book hoarder."

"I am not!"

"You are," Sophie replied, coaxing Iris onto her back with a palm on her shoulder. All the gentle ways Sophie touched her suddenly had a new, more intimate meaning. How much control and effort she must use to control her strength, it aroused Iris in an instant, like a head rush. "But as part of my penance, I promise not to say a single word about your book purchases for at least one full fiscal year. Deal?"

Had any blood remained in her brain, Iris might've negotiated better terms. Instead she replied with a breathless, "Deal."

Later that night, cozied in bed with Chloe at their feet, Sophie rested her head on Iris's shoulder as Iris happily made a purchase from their local bookstore on her phone. After successfully getting through checkout, she turned her screen off and put the phone on the bedside table. Wrapping her arm around Sophie, she enjoyed the closeness of her and the calm thump of their tandem heartbeats.

Sophie inhaled sharply. "Did you just order *three* box s—"

"I ordered three box sets of books, yes."
"Okay."

Publisher's note: Look for Beyond the Blue, *the debut novel from author TJ O'Shea coming out in 2022 from Bella Books.*

THE WAY WE WERE

Regina Jamison

My eyes opened to slits as I threw the comforter off of my chest and down toward my waist. The heat of the day had already invaded the bedroom and an overwhelming feeling of warmth had engulfed me.

I stretched like a lioness—pelvis thrusted forward, toes curled under, butt cheeks squeezed tight—and let out an obnoxiously loud sound. Grace, who was on the bed beside me, reached her hand back and gently patted my waist. For a moment, I was slightly panicked as I went through the days of the week in my head, but then the calm feeling of relief came over me as I recalled that it was Saturday. The COVID-19 pandemic lockdown and having to work remotely from home had blurred one day into the next like a summer vacation. My lower back and butt were sore from sitting at a computer all day teaching students on Zoom and Google Meet, so I had started doing yoga with Rodney Yee on YouTube. I was grateful for every "Downward Facing Dog" and "Pigeon-pose" Rodney guided me through.

"Hey sleepyhead," I called over to Grace. "Are you going to hit the yoga mat with me today?"

Grace sighed and rolled onto her back. The deep bronze color of her skin had paled from lack of sun. New Yorkers had been forced into a lockdown because of the COVID-19 virus. Trips to the store to get food and scarce supplies were, now, the only times we ventured outside. Masks, pressed into our faces to cover our mouths and our noses, were the new fashion accessory. Grace and I decided to lockdown together. We figured that quarantining ourselves from the rest of the Bronx in my condo apartment was better than quarantining alone.

"Yoga? No, I'm good," Grace said as she sat up in bed, reached for her phone on the nightstand, and tapped in her passcode.

"Well, I need to work out and stretch. I feel like I've definitely gained weight."

"You look lovely, Sky. It's just a little extra for me to hold on to. I love it."

I smiled, but I threw my pillow at Grace and said, "Gee, thanks!"

"Forecast says eighty-one degrees today," Grace said.

"Well, it is May 30th. June is right around the corner. I can't wait for school to be over!"

"Tired of being chained to the computer all day, huh?"

"A little, but I like working remotely. Now I have so many platforms available to me that I can use to reach my students. We really should've been using all of these things before, but I guess most of the students didn't have laptops or iPads, so that would have been impossible. One thing this pandemic has brought to light is the inequities within the education system."

"How so?"

"Schools with money, aka, schools located in richer neighborhoods fell into remote learning seamlessly. In fact, many of these schools had already been engaged in remote learning. Schools in neighborhoods that are less endowed, like my school, got hit by the lockdown the hardest. My school struggled. Teachers had to learn on the fly. We all became IT specialists overnight. It was rough, but we didn't quit, and we learned some resumé-worthy skills along the way. Definitely grateful for that!"

"Amen. Take those skills and run with them, but, yeah, I know what you mean. With the masks covering people's faces and no interpreters present to interpret during the White House briefing about COVID, it's been very hard for the Deaf and Hard-of-Hearing communities as well."

"Why haven't there been any interpreters?"

"White House keeps blocking the requests. They think it's not important which is totally crazy."

"Jerks!" I yelled. "Let's just hope and pray folks really get out there and vote on election day so we can get that pompous ass that's in the White House now, out."

"Amen, again!"

Grace's phone vibrated. "Oh, I need to take this. FaceTime call with Lydia. She needs an interpreter for her upcoming appointment with her kid's teacher."

"Okay. I'll be downstairs."

The living room was warm and stuffy. I cracked the windows to about two inches then went into the kitchen and did the same to the window in there. Our main respite during the pandemic was the small, private yard that came with the condo. I put on my mask, unlocked, and pushed open the sliding glass door that separated the dining room from the backyard, and stepped outside onto the top step. The city, or rather, the nation, had been locked down for about three months now and in that time it seemed that nature had flourished. The trees seemed greener and fuller. More butterflies than I had ever seen before took to landing and perching on the roses in my rose bush to flutter their wings and show off their exquisite patterns. And recently, just before dusk, what seemed like hundreds of Starlings took to the sky to perform beautifully intricate murmuration patterns that were out of this world.

I stood on the step and looked around. My yard was private, but my neighbors on both sides yards bordered my own. The neighbor on the left, Carmen Sanchez, had fled the city a few days after COVID hit. She said she was headed to the Dominican Republic to be with her family. How I longed to go with her. A deserted beach, a turquoise-blue sea, and some extreme sun and heat were definitely things I dreamt about since the pandemic happened. The neighbor on the right, Karen Powell, was still at home, but she wasn't one to sit outside much, so we didn't see much of her.

I stood on the step for awhile as I looked at my backyard and thought about the items I should go back inside to get to clean the small, round table and three chairs I had out there when Grace stepped through the opened sliding door. She stood behind me, held me around my waist, and nuzzled my neck. I felt the soft fabric of her mask against my skin. I turned my head to look at her. She was wearing a black mask that had the letters B-L-M appliquéd onto the center of the mask in fuzzy, golden, large capital letters. B-L-M was for Black Lives Matter. We had just taken part in a march two days ago to protest the killing of George Floyd, police brutality, institutional racism, and everything else evil in America that affected our lives and the lives of those we helped and educated and cared about. The protest we attended was peaceful and remained so, but the Google News updates that came in on our phones informed us that other protests and protesters weren't as lucky.

"Did you square everything away with Lydia?" I asked Grace. Then I turned my attention back to the yard, back to the table and chairs that needed cleaning.

"Yes, she finally found the time and date the teacher told her, so we are set for Wednesday at ten thirty."

"That's good."

"I spoke to Ola."

"What's going on with her? How's she making out?"

"She's stuck in London."

"WHAT!"

"Yeah, she was doing an art show in London when the pandemic hit and now that they aren't allowing folks to travel, she's stuck."

"Oh my goodness!"

"She says she has a lot of friends there, so she'll manage."

"Well that's good."

"Ola told me that she spoke to Suzy."

"Suzy? Who's Suzy?"

"You know the bartender at Pandora's. She made that delicious drink for us that she named Suzy Sunshine."

"Oh, yes. Ola and Suzy are friends like that?"

"Apparently. I never knew that, but I guess they are. Anyway, Suzy told Ola that Pandora's has closed down."

"WHAT!"

"Yup. The landlord couldn't pay the rent. Another casualty of the pandemic. I'm telling you this whole thing is really starting to feel like we're living in a dystopian novel or something. Totally unbelievable."

"Yeah, I know," I replied and squeezed her arms tighter around my waist. "How are your parents doing? Did you call them today? How's Hope and her new girlfriend?" I asked as I rolled my eyes a little. Hope and I still had our issues, but things had gotten a bit better since she'd found the new love of her life to keep her busy and out of Grace's business.

"My parents are good. They're staying at my grandparent's house in New Paltz."

"Lucky them."

"Yeah, and Hope and Hilda are doing great. At least that's what Hope says."

"Hope and Hilda. H and H. Sounds like a brand name."

Grace chuckled, "Yes, it does. Maybe they'll start a business."

I turned around to face Grace. "I know some business I'd like to start."

Grace pulled me deeper into her arms. "Oh, yeah, and what business is that?"

"Come with me upstairs and I'll show you," I coyly teased as I slipped around Grace and made my way through the opened glass sliding door.

Grace slapped my ass, and I could tell she was smiling behind her mask because her eyes were squished into narrow slits.

"I'm right behind you," Grace said.

After our sexual escapade had concluded, I finally cleaned the table and chairs in the backyard and Grace and I sat to eat our midday meal.

"So, what else is on the agenda for today?" Grace asked. A sly smile on her face.

I scoffed. "There's not much else we can do. Social distancing remember."

"We didn't social distance during the march the other day. Oh, wait, I take that back. We were very careful to keep our distance from the throngs of people thanks to your reminders."

"You are very welcome," I said, then I bit into a piece of cinnamon raisin toast slathered with vegan butter and topped with blue agave sweetener.

"I know. Let's go for a bike ride. We can social distance and take in the sights at the same time," Grace said.

"That, my dear, sounds like a great plan."

I chugged down the rest of my orange-mango juice, wiped my mouth, and began gathering plates, knives, forks, and napkins. Grace swiped up the glasses and used a combination of hips and feet to push the chairs back under the round glass table. Then we took everything inside.

For my birthday, Grace had bought me a new bike that matched her own—black frame and tires, three speeds, and Gator Skin covering over the tires to prevent punctures. The two differences were my bike had a black, wire mesh basket at the front of the bike where hers was at the back of her bike and my bike had straight handlebars, hers had handlebars turned up like bull horns. I was lucky she'd bought me the bike when she did because now, since the pandemic, bikes had become scarce since everyone started riding as it was a way to be outside and social distance at the same time and bike prices had soared.

We pedaled toward the greenway trail at Leland Avenue near the Soundview Park Salt Marsh Restoration—masks on, helmets off, hair and earrings swaying in the breeze—and followed the trail edged with patches of tall grasses that looked long, yellowed, and wispy further along the greenway. We were the only people around.

"Wow, no one else is here," I yelled back at Grace who was on the trail behind me. "I thought there'd be more people on the trail today."

Grace pedaled a little faster and pulled up beside me. "Just us. Let's stop for a few at the rocks near the water."

"Okay," I said.

Along the trail there was an area that had big, square, concrete blocks that overlooked the water. I wasn't sure if the water in that particular area contained water from the Long Island Sound or the Hudson River, but whatever it was, it was peaceful. We leaned our bikes against an empty bench and sat on another empty bench that was beside it. Since no one else was around we took off our masks. The air smelled clean, cleaner than it had smelled before and the scent of wildflowers perfumed the air. Every few seconds we witnessed a squirrel or two jumping down from a tree in search of nuts or one who had found her leftover stash and was intent on digging it up and eating it.

"It's so nice here," I said. I sat, snuggled under Grace's right arm, my left hand on her left thigh. Her right arm hung loosely around my neck.

"It sure is," Grace replied and at the same time, we both filled our lungs with the cleaner air and breathed out all of our worries and stress.

"Maybe things will be different now that so many issues have been brought to light like police brutality, racism, sexism, global warming. I mean, it's obvious to me that since there have been less cars on the road and less factories spewing pollution into the air due to pandemic closures that the air is cleaner, and nature is making a comeback."

"Yeah, true, but people see what they want to see. They see the things that benefit them. You see how they're rushing and hoping to get things back to the way they were without considering that maybe the way things were is not something we should rush back to. People don't want to change. Especially when they feel like their place in society is being challenged. They act like there's not enough for everybody, but there is."

"Maybe we should move to Costa Rica," I said. The deserted beaches and turquoise-blue ocean I'd thought about earlier today were still on my mind. The weather was getting warmer and the wanderlust that always hit me when the temperatures reached eighty degrees or higher was beginning to overtake me.

"Get a nice house on the beach with a firepit and a huge deck that faces the ocean," Grace said.

"Watch the waves and the storms roll in," I added.

"Work from home. You'd have your office and I'd have mine," Grace replied.

I untangled myself from under her arm, sat up, and kissed her. When we pulled away, I stared into Grace's golden eyes and said, "We should do it."

"Really?" Grace questioned. "We should just pack up our stuff and hightail it to Costa Rica? What about travel restrictions? What about our families and friends? What about your mom and dad and brother?"

"We'll find a way around travel restrictions and my family will be fine. They're doing everything they're supposed to do to stay safe and besides, this is the perfect opportunity to do something different, live differently. Off the grid, but not really off the grid since the pandemic has sort of brought the whole world together via Zoom, right. I mean, right now, we really have become a global village. Let's take advantage of it!"

Grace looked at me for a moment then she smiled and said, "Okay, let's do it!"

I kissed Grace hard on the mouth then I jumped up and did a little dance as I chanted, "We're moving to Costa Rica! We're moving to Costa Rica!" Grace laughed.

"Come on," Grace said, getting up from the bench. "Let's ride some more. Get that exercise that you've been craving."

"Maybe we can find a place with a pool in Costa Rica then I can swim whenever I want!"

"That would be awesome," Grace said.

I got on my bike, reached into my backpack that was in the basket at the front of my bike, and pulled out my water bottle. The sun was hot. It felt good on my face and skin, but it made me thirsty. I gulped down the cold water and wiped my mouth with my sleeve. Grace mounted her bike, adjusted her sunglasses, and smiled at me.

"You know this is crazy, right," Grace said.

"I know," I replied and gave her what I hoped was a reassuring smile.

"But I want you to know it feels right because I'm doing it with you, Sky Valentine. I'd go anywhere with you."

"I love you too, Grace," I said and walked my bike over to hers and gave her a long, deep kiss.

"Okay," Grace said when our kiss was done. "Let's move it, babe! A couple more laps around then home to pack!"

"Costa Rica, here we come!" I yelled as we made our way further along the deserted trail.

The characters in this short story first appeared in the novel Choosing Grace *by Regina Jamison.* Choosing Grace *is available from Bella Books or your favorite retailer.*

SIX FEET AWAY

Jamie Anderson

Frustrated, these walls don't say much
I miss my friends, I miss human touch
There's still a world outside
Through the darkness there is light

Take a walk, the sun is warm
Feel myself transform
Summer's coming, a gorgeous day
You're still beautiful from six feet away

Some don't believe, they think it's a lie
I have to let that go, hope they don't die
I say a prayer and close my eyes
Picture the beauty of a clear blue sky

Take a walk, the sun is warm
Feel myself transform
Summer's coming, a gorgeous day
You're still beautiful from two metres away

When this is over our lives may change
Remember that sunny day, even if it rains

Take a walk, the sun is warm
Feel yourself transform
Spring is coming, a gorgeous day
We're all beautiful from six feet away
Two metres away

© 2020 Jamie Anderson
Available on *Songs from Home*, Tsunami Recordings, Jamie Anderson

AT OUR AGE

KG MacGregor

Louise Stevens tapped the floor to swing her hanging basket chair, a present from Marty for her seventy-eighth birthday. The cushions and pillows inside made it perfect for reading or streaming a TV show on her tablet computer. Or for video chats like this one with her best friend Linda.

"Be honest, Lou. It's Charlie you miss most, not me," Linda said, a reference to her Cavalier King Charles spaniel.

"I do miss that little rascal. He helps fill the hole Petie left." Her beloved Boston terrier had lived a nice long life, fifteen spoiled rotten years. "Marty keeps saying we ought to get another dog but it just doesn't seem right. If he lives as long as Petie, why…we'd be in our nineties! I wouldn't want the poor fella to lose his mamas and have to go to the shelter."

"They say the shelters are almost empty. People are lonely at home and now they have more time for pets."

"I read that in the paper," Louise said. She hoped those people realized pets were forever and didn't abandon them once this COVID-19 mess was over. "How are you doing in the lonely department?"

"You don't have to worry about me on my own, Lou. I've had nine years to get used to it."

It was hard to believe Shirley had been gone that long. Louise had almost died of loneliness after losing Rhonda, but then golf pro Marty Beck came along and gave her a reason to live and love again. Linda was content with Charlie and the cats, three of them at last count.

"I know you're used to it but this is all so different, not being able to see our friends or go out to eat, or even walk on the beach. I feel so lucky I have Marty or I'd be going crazy."

Every day was a crap shoot in Southwest Florida with county commissioners saying one thing and the governor saying something else. Marty and Louise had decided for themselves that protecting one another meant staying home as much as possible and following the strictest of guidelines when they absolutely had to go out.

They'd settled into their individual routines since their lockdown began, Louise with her books and crosswords, and Marty with her jigsaw puzzles. Daily calisthenics in the pool and the occasional walk through the neighborhood provided exercise, though Louise still found walks sad without Petie.

"How's Marty doing?"

Louise sighed. "She's okay, I guess. I caught her crying a little the other day, but that's to be expected. She worked with Bennie for forty-odd years, even way back in Michigan."

"He was my age, you know. Eighty-one. It really brings it home when it's somebody you know. They say he was out on the golf course on Friday and by Tuesday he was gone."

"And we couldn't even have a funeral. This virus, Linda… it's coming for us old people. Especially people with underlying health conditions. You know, Bennie smoked all those years."

"Too many birthdays is an underlying health condition," Linda replied drolly. "What I can't stand is how they talk about us on TV like we're just numbers. Ten thousand, fifty thousand, a hundred thousand. We're people's partners and friends."

And in Marty's case, mother and grandmother. "Katie calls every day asking if there's anything we need. She thought I'd have to tie Marty up to keep her in the house, but it turns out I'm the one with cabin fever. I miss going to the library and out to lunch with you and Pauline. Of course we both miss golf but we're not allowed to talk about that anymore."

Poor Marty had worked her way back from a knee replacement at seventy-one only to tear her rotator cuff, effectively ending her career as the club pro at the Pine Island Country Club. Her attempts to play a leisurely round always ended with excruciating pain that lasted for days. When the kinks in her neck got worse, she finally called it quits, donating all her golf gear to the recreation center. As a show of solidarity, Louise did the same.

"Too bad y'ins sold your house in the mountains, Lou. A change of scenery sure would be nice this summer. It's getting hotter every day."

"We'd just be trading one set of four walls for another. Besides, the last thing Marty wants is to sit on a deck and watch other people play golf."

They'd sold their North Carolina home with hopes of traveling a bit while they could still carry a suitcase. A fall drive through New England, a bus and train tour through the Southwest. Their Barcelona-to-Venice cruise, which they'd been looking forward to for years, had been canceled as thousands of passengers languished at sea in search of a port that would accept them.

"Is Marty keeping busy?"

"Right now she's at the dining room table working a two thousand-piece puzzle of Niagara Falls. That's why I'm sitting out here on the lanai, because every time she adds a piece, she calls me over to see."

"Bless her heart. You should give her an M&M."

"Just what she needs—two thousand M&Ms. I'd never get her up from the table." They shared a laugh at Marty's expense. "We've got a feast coming tonight, one of those delivery apps. It's like takeout except somebody else goes and gets it. Marty's been craving a basket of fried oysters. Doesn't that sound good? I always get mine with Cajun fries but she likes the sweet potato fries."

Linda made a face and visibly shuddered. "I don't know how y'ins eat those nasty things. Shirley used to eat them raw, right out of the shell. A live animal sliding down your throat!"

"The ones we get are cooked and they're delicious. I'll save you one. I can stick it in an envelope and drop it in the mail."

"Don't you dare!"

Louise laughed and dragged her foot to stop the swinging chair. "I probably should go in there and express my amazement at how many pieces she's managed to fit together. You want to have dinner with us on Tuesday? Virtual, I mean. We can make that Greek salad with the bowtie pasta and pepperoni. Everybody likes that."

"It's a date. Just let me know what time to be ready."

"All righty, you give King Charles a scratch from us."

Louise entered the house through the master bedroom so she could brush her hair and touch up her lipstick. After fifteen years together, she still liked looking nice for Marty.

"Hi there, beautiful," Marty said, looking up from her puzzle with an appreciative smile.

"Hi yourself, cutie pie." Louise threaded her fingers through Marty's short, textured locks, taking a moment to appreciate her handiwork. Marty had stopped coloring her hair not long after her knee replacement, going from ash blond to ash gray, and hardly anyone noticed. "This cut turned out nice, if I must say so myself."

"I'll be sure to pass that on to my incredibly talented stylist. How's Linda?"

"She's fine, but I worry about her being there all by herself for so long. What would you think about us having her over? For real, I mean. She hasn't been out of that house for a month except to walk Charlie. Gets everything delivered, just like us. We could make our own little three-person bubble."

Marty's smile faded. "I don't know, Lou. I guess it's safe… but it wouldn't feel right. I can't even see my own grandson.

What am I supposed to tell Katie and Tyler if we let Linda come over but not them?"

"Katie and Tyler aren't shut up in their house like we are. Tyler's out on a construction project every day with a dozen other men. We don't know if they wear masks or go out for a beer after work. And Katie does all our shopping and hers too. She sees people and handles stuff. Now she's taking over the clubhouse from Bennie. I know she's careful, but all it takes is one little mistake. People like us, Marty…at our age one little mistake can be deadly." She read the disappointment on Marty's face. "But I promise we'll find a way to be with them. Maybe when they open the beaches again, we can all meet over on Sanibel for a walk on the beach. They say it's a lot safer outside."

"Yeah, maybe." She sounded glum.

"Honey, what's wrong? Come sit with me."

Marty dutifully rose from the table and followed Louise to the couch, where they sat side by side holding hands. "It's these crazy times, Lou. And crazy people. I went to post a note on Bennie's Facebook page for his family, and some idiot was saying how he played golf with Bennie last week, that he was living life to the fullest…standing up to the virus instead of hiding at home. Does he not realize this stupid virus *killed* him? What kind of moron thumps his chest about that? Makes me weep for all of humanity."

"Or at least for the education system," Louise said wryly. "Those people think staying home and wearing masks out makes us cowards."

"*Pfft!* What's that old saying? 'I'd rather be a live coward than a dead hero.' That's me. And it's true—I really am a coward. I'm afraid if I go out there, I'll catch this bug and bring it home to you. If something happened to you, Lou…that would just be the end of the world."

"Oh, Marty." Louise wrapped her in a hug, squeezing hard enough that she accidentally made something in her shoulder pop. "Oh no, did I hurt you?"

"Heck no! If I can't see my chiropractor, you're the next best thing."

* * *

"Eight...nine...ten. Now the left leg," Marty said as they completed their daily calisthenics in the small pool. While it wasn't big enough for swimming, it was perfect for cooling off and keeping their joints limber with these simple resistance exercises. "I like doing these leg lifts, Lou. Feels good on my you-know-what."

Louise laughed. "I knew you were going to say that."

"That's why I don't wear a swimsuit. Every time I raise my leg, it smiles like a kid with a birthday cake."

"You don't wear a swimsuit because you think it's funny to moon Bob Shackleton. I bet he's over there right now with his binoculars waiting for you to get out."

They'd long suspected their backdoor neighbor across the canal was spying on them through their windows and screens. Louise confirmed it one day, peering from the bedroom with her own binoculars while Marty was in the pool.

"Come on, Lou. You have to appreciate a guy who gets off looking at a seventy-six-year-old butt with more dimples than a golf ball. Let's ask Barbara when Bob's birthday is so we can moon him at the same time. Wouldn't that be a great present?"

"Unless we gave him a heart attack." Louise skimmed across the pool and wrapped her arms around Marty. "I happen to like looking at your butt too. What does that say about me?"

"It says that you, like Bob, have very good taste."

"You're the one that tastes good," Louise demurred.

"Oooh, I love it when you talk dirty."

Five sharp beeps from the kitchen signaled the end of their aquacise now that their coffee was finished brewing. Marty shamelessly shook her butt as she climbed out of the pool, knowing it would make Louise laugh again.

She took her time showering poolside behind a screen Louise had insisted she erect. By the time she'd dried off and dressed in her trademark baggy shorts and Hawaiian shirt, Louise was in the kitchen making breakfast.

"Bacon and eggs?" Marty asked.

"Bran flakes and blueberries."

"Yum! I was so hoping you'd say that." She even said it with enthusiasm, though both of them knew it wasn't true. Left to her own devices, Marty likely would have clogged her arteries by now and added heart bypass surgery to her growing list of emergency fixes. Louise fed her healthy meals at home, limiting their extravagances to a few times a month, like the fried oysters they'd enjoyed a week ago. "In case I haven't told you lately, I feel very lucky to have you taking care of me."

"That's because I want to keep you around for a long time."

"Good, because you'd have a heck of a time getting rid of me."

As Louise poured their coffee, Marty wrapped her arms around her from behind. She'd begun to worry that the isolation was taking a toll on Louise. She was listless, leaving her book every half hour to wander the house and look out the windows. She'd rearranged drawers and closets, sometimes more than once. Then yesterday, Marty had found her in the den poring over the cruise brochures, lamenting the trip they'd had to cancel.

"We'll get another crack at that Mediterranean cruise, Lou. We just have to wait this thing out."

Louise's face fell at the mention of the cruise. "I feel cheated, Marty. We worked hard and saved our money, took care of our health so we could enjoy this part of our life. Now it's been snatched away from us and there may not be time to get it back. We'll be that much older, that much more feeble. By the time we're allowed to do things again, we won't be able to."

"Sweetheart, listen." Marty took both mugs from Louise and set them on the counter so they could embrace. "I get what you mean about being cheated out of the cruise, just like I feel cheated that Tyler's about to become a dad and I won't be able to hold my great-grandson for who knows how long. But torturing ourselves over what we don't have is a waste of time and energy. Let's talk about we *can* do. You and me. Because here's the gods' honest truth, Lou. I'd rather be stuck here in the house with you than anywhere in the world with somebody else."

"Marty, my darling." Louise kissed her on the forehead, nose and lips. "I don't feel cheated when it comes to you. What I feel is lucky that I get to have you all to myself."

"That's great, honey. I feel the same way. So all we have to do now is make this time special. Are you up for it?"

"Absolutely. How should we do that?"

"Well…if it were up to me, I'd start with bacon and eggs."

* * *

Louise twirled in her hanging chair, where she kept one eye on Marty at the dining room table and the other on Bob Shackleton, who was trimming the bushes in his backyard, no doubt for a clearer view of Marty in her birthday suit as she climbed in and out of the pool.

Linda had stepped away from their video chat to fetch Charlie so Louise could say hello. She returned empty-handed. "Sorry, Lou. He's in the middle of my bed zonked out. They could do surgery on him right now and he wouldn't budge."

"I'm sure it's tiring being that cute all the time," Louise said. "Marty's got something up her sleeve. I have no idea what it is but she's been sneaky all day, talking on the phone and texting with somebody. She's like a schoolgirl passing notes."

"Maybe she got you a present. Don't you two have an anniversary coming up?"

"Not for three more weeks. We're going to order chateaubriand for two from the Veranda and lay out a romantic candlelight dinner. Marty wants us to move the living room furniture back so we can dance."

"That sounds lovely. How many is this?"

"Five since the wedding, fifteen since we moved in together." In fact they'd chosen that wedding date because it was the day they'd also celebrated becoming a committed couple.

"It's nice you and Marty got to marry here in Florida. Our wedding was sweet there on the dock in P-Town, but Shirley used to say she didn't feel married once we got back home."

"I remember what she said about the drive back, that she had to keep checking the GPS to see if you were married."

In fact Louise had invoked Shirley's rationale to hold Marty's marriage proposal at bay, knowing full well she'd be boxed in if the Supreme Court made it the law of the land. Privately, she'd told herself it wouldn't be fair to Rhonda because they'd spent thirty years together and never had the chance to marry. If she were honest though, she probably wouldn't have had the nerve to marry Rhonda even if same-sex marriage had been legal back then. Her insistence on privacy—which she later came to admit was her own internalized homophobia—had kept her in the closet for most of her life. After serious soul searching, she concluded that Rhonda would have been proud of the strides she'd made with Marty, the ultimate stride being to stand in front of their friends on the 18th green at Pine Island and make a public commitment to be Marty's wife.

"I ought to go in there and swipe her phone, see who she's been texting with."

"Don't do that, Lou. If she's planning a surprise, you'll spoil it."

"Oh, I wouldn't really. Half the fun is knowing she's up to something. We've been trying to come up with ways to entertain each other. I found a word search puzzle yesterday that was all golf terms, so I made her a copy and we had a contest to see who could find them all first. We both kept getting louder and crazier. I was almost finished and I want you to know she grabbed my pencil and threw it in the living room. By the time I found it and got back, she was finished."

Laughing along with her, Linda finally caught her breath. "That's what I miss most, Lou—how silly we all get when we play games. I can't wait till we can be together again for laughs like that."

"Same here, my friend."

Louise decided not to mention that she and Marty had talked it over and agreed to invite Linda into their bubble. She wanted to give it a couple more days to be sure Marty had thought it through and wasn't doing it just to appease her.

"Uh-oh, Marty's gone to look out the front window. Something's definitely up, Linda. I'd better go see what it is. We'll talk later. Love you!"

Marty cut her off at the door between the lanai and their bedroom. "Honey, I have a surprise for you…a good one, I hope. But you have to stay in here till I call you. No peeking."

"I *knew* you were up to something! You sneaky thing."

It was almost five o'clock, the time Louise usually started making dinner. They hadn't talked all day about what to have, so it made perfect sense Marty had ordered something special. Come to think of it, she'd mentioned a couple of days ago that she hadn't had barbecue in forever. A rib feast for two from Rib City would be a perfect surprise.

She heard Marty go out the front door and come back in.

"Stay in there, Lou. No peeking."

"I'm not peeking." But her mouth was watering.

After a couple of minutes, Marty called, "Okay, put your mask on."

Her mask? Surely Marty hadn't invited someone into their home without asking her. The only one they'd discussed was Linda. It couldn't be her because she was on the video chat only moments ago sitting out by her pool.

"Are you ready?"

"Hold on." She tamped down her irritation, knowing she'd have to be sociable with their guest, whoever it was. "All right."

Marty opened the door a crack and slithered in—without a mask. "Great! Now pull that mask up so it covers your eyes."

"A blindfold?"

"That's right. Now take my hand."

She stepped carefully past the threshold, the fingertips of her free hand running along the wall until it ended at the living room. Whatever this surprise was, it didn't smell like barbecue. In fact, it didn't smell like anything.

"Just a few more steps." Marty led her to a space on the couch. "Okay, sit right there."

Louise heard her walk across the room to pick up something, then return to sit next to her.

"Here goes nothing, Lou. Go ahead and take your mask off."

"Let's see what you've—" Her heart melted instantly at the sight of a full-grown, big-eyed Boston terrier quivering with fright. Unlike Petie, who had a white face with a black patch over one eye, this dog's markings were symmetrical and his coat was brindle instead of black. "Oh, my goodness gracious!"

"Say hello to Archie."

"Archie." When a soft scratch to Archie's chin did nothing to calm the poor pup's tremors, Louise scooped him into her lap and continued to stroke him. "Marty, where on earth…"

"It's complicated. Remember that call I got this morning while you were getting dressed? It was Dr. Gray." Kevin Gray was Petie's longtime veterinarian. "He asked if we were interested in another Boston terrier. I told him we talked about it, that we didn't think it was a good idea to take on another at our age because we might not be around to take care of him. But Archie, he's eight years old. And a real mama's boy, Dr. Gray said."

Louise could tell that from the way Archie had settled in her lap. His trembling had almost subsided as he lay down and accepted the same gentle caresses Louise had used to calm Petie during a thunderstorm.

"Archie's owner died last Monday…some kind of cancer."

"Bless their little hearts!"

"She was a teacher like you—third grade, I think he said— till a couple of years ago when she got sick. Her son works construction in Alaska, says he can't take care of a dog right now. Dr. Gray thought since we lost Petie…well, he was hoping we'd consider keeping him for a few days to see how we all got along. I know I should have asked you first but…"

"Marty," Louise said plaintively. There was no point in scolding her about doing this behind her back. She might have said no and missed out on the chance to bring darling Archie into their life.

"We won't have him a long time like Petie, but a few good years would mean a lot to this little guy. Dr. Gray says it's hard finding homes for senior dogs. He's always been a good boy, but now he's just scared and lonely. I thought we'd make a nice family."

The little fella had curled himself into a ball, his nose buried beneath his hind leg.

"You deliberately attacked my weakness"—Louise couldn't stop her smile—"and obviously it worked. He owns my heart already. Of course we'll keep him."

Marty broke into a satisfied grin. "Thank God. I was hoping you'd say that. Isn't he adorable?"

"He's a precious boy. Aren't you, Archie? Just a precious little boy." He flattened his ears and wiggled his nubby tail in response to her singsong voice. "Aww, look at him. Eight years old. He'll keep us in shape, won't he? Two walks a day will be good for all three of us."

His head shot up at the familiar word, and he looked from one to the other.

"Look at him, Marty. He even understands the W-word, just like Petie."

"I sneaked out to the garage earlier and got Petie's harness and leash. Shall I do the honors?" As she started to rise, Louise caught her shirt to tug her back.

"I love you, you...sneaky, conniving...dearest sweetheart. I didn't even know I needed Archie but you did."

"What I know"—Marty curled a hand around Louise's neck and leaned in to rub noses—"is this little boy needs somebody to love him like his mama did. You have so much love in your heart, Lou. It spills out everywhere you go."

Louise had always been helpless against Marty's silver tongue. She nuzzled Archie again and said, "I hope you're ready for more, both of you. Because every day I wake up beside you, my love just gets bigger and bigger. I'm the luckiest woman in the world."

She followed Marty's eyes to the window, where a car had pulled into their driveway.

"You're about to get even luckier," Marty said, licking her lips. "Since I also ordered us some barbecued ribs."

The characters in this short story first appeared in the novel Mulligan *by KG MacGregor.* Mulligan *is available from Bella Books or your favorite retailer.*

About the Authors

Jamie Anderson

Jamie Anderson has worn out three pickup trucks since 1987, seen forty-seven of fifty states, immigrated to Canada, and consumed countless cases of M&M's while bringing her brand of confused folk music to venues around the world. The award winning composer and musician taught herself guitar by memorizing chords in a Mel Bay song book. She now teaches guitar, mandolin, ukulele, and songwriting in her studio and for schools. A native of Arizona, she lives in Ottawa.

Kat Jackson

Kat is a high school English teacher living in Pennsylvania who has been buried in and under books for thirty-some years. A lifelong learner, Kat currently has two masters degrees: one in English Literature, and another in Clinical & Counseling Psychology, plus an unofficial degree in true crime podcasts. She puts far too much stock into words and has been writing since she was twelve years old. Kat is an avid collector of books, typewriters, feelings, and beat-up running shoes that carry miles of self-preservation. And also: cats.

Regina Jamison

Regina Jamison is a writer who lives in Brooklyn, New York. Her poetry has appeared in several literary journals among them are, *Sinister Wisdom: Black Lesbian Revolution*, *Five Two One Magazine*, and *Magma Literary Journal: Deaf Issue*, *The Americas Poetry Festival of New York Anthology 2016*, *Promethean Literary Journal*, *Off the Rocks: An Anthology of GLBT Writing Vols. 14 & 15*, and *Poetry in Performance Journal Vol. 43*. Online, her poetry has appeared in *Gnashing Teeth Journal*, *Silver Birch Press — Me as a Child Series*, *The Lake Literary Journal*, and *Mom Egg Review*. Her poems will also appear in the upcoming issue of *Switchgrass Review*. Her short stories have appeared in *Girls Who Bite: Vampire Lesbian Anthology*, *Zane's Purple Panties*, and the *Lambda Literary Anthology: Gaslight*. She is a Guest Editor for *Gnashing Teeth Journal*'s upcoming anthology, *SHE: Seen. Heard. Engaged*. She received her MFA in Creative Writing at City College in New York. Her first novel, *Choosing Grace*, has been published by Bella Books.

J. E. Knowles

J. E. Knowles was "born in the U.S.A., made in Canada." Her novels are *The Trees in the Field* and *Arusha*, a Lambda Literary Award finalist. She is also the editor of *Faith in Writing*, a book of essays.

RJ Layer

RJ Layer resides in the "Heart" of the Midwest with her partner and new wife, of over twenty-five years, and their two feline rescues. She is a certified romance nut, and loves writing lesbian romance. In addition to traveling to new places, RJ can be found relaxing in the rolling hills on the water. Their hideaway is the perfect place for dreaming up engaging characters and moving stories. She's also quite passionate about photography and reading every free minute she can find.

KG MacGregor

Though she'd always dreamed of becoming an astronaut, KG MacGregor earned her PhD in journalism and went to work as a political pollster and market researcher. In 2002, she began writing fanfiction for the *Xena:Warrior Princess* fandom and discovered her bliss. Since then, she has authored over two dozen novels, collecting a Lammy and nine Golden Crown Awards. KG is past-president of the Board of Trustees of the Lambda Literary Foundation. A native of the North Carolina mountains, she now makes her home in Nashville, TN with her partner Jenny, and two raucous felines, Rozzie and Agnes.

Lise MacTague

Lise MacTague is a hockey player, a librarian, and an author. Her parents had their priorities straight and introduced her to sci-fi at the age of three through reruns of *Star Trek*. Lise has been an overworked art student, a freelance artist, a Rennie, a slave to retail, a grad student, and a slinger of beer. She lives in Milwaukee with two very demanding cats, one who is curled up in her lap even now.

Catherine Maiorisi

Catherine Maiorisi is the author of the NYPD Detective Chiara Corelli mystery series featuring Corelli and her reluctant partner, Detective P.J. Parker. The first two books in the series, *A Matter of Blood* and *The Blood Runs Cold* were Lambda Literary Award finalists. The third, *A Message in Blood*, was published in January 2021. When she wrote a short story to create the backstory for the love interest in the Corelli mysteries, Catherine had never read any romance and hadn't considered writing it. To her surprise, "The Fan Club" turned out to be a romance and was included in the Best Lesbian Romance of 2014 edited by Radclyffe. Since then, Catherine has published four romance novels: *Matters of the Heart, No One But You, Ready for Love* and *Taking a Chance on Love*. She is an active member of Sisters in Crime, Mystery Writers of America and The Golden Crown Literary Society. Visit Catherine at www.catherinemaiorisi.com.

TJ O'Shea

TJ O'Shea is a New Jerseyian by location and a New Yorker by vocation. When not working in the video game industry or writing angsty queer romances, she enjoys playing video games (this time for fun), shouting answers at *Jeopardy!* reruns, amateurishly baking, spending time with her wife and singing to their cat. TJ's first novel *Beyond the Blue* will be released by Bella Books in 2022.

Melissa Price

Melissa is a novelist, who in the absence of computer or pen, isn't too proud to write in crayon or spray paint. Her works include the exciting romantic intrigue novels *Steel Eyes*, and *Skin in the Game* (a *Steel Eyes* midquel). Melissa's works-in-progress are a sociopolitical farce titled *The Right Closet*, and an untitled lesbian romance based on her short story, *The Desert Diner*, which was included in the Bella Books anthology *Happily Ever After*. A retired Doctor of Chiropractic and a lifelong guitarist, she also co-wrote the authorized biographical screenplay, *Toma—The Man, The Mission, The Message*. While her house is in Phoenix, Arizona, Melissa lives between some un-named exotic Caribbean island and Paris's Left Bank.

Tracey Richardson

Tracey Richardson came to a love of books early on, thanks to a mother who took her and her two siblings regularly to the library in the Windsor area of Ontario, Canada, just across the river from Detroit. She even loves the smell of the ink and paper in books and to this day, when she opens a brand new book, she always gives it a good sniff! A journalist by trade, she worked at Ontario daily newspapers as first a reporter and later a copy editor. Semi-retired now, she finally has more time to devote to her fiction writing.

Ann Roberts

Ann Roberts is the award-winning author of twenty romance, mystery and general fiction novels, including the Ari Adams mystery series. She has been short-listed for a Lambda Literary Award three times, and she has the unusual distinction of being recognized in both the Mystery and Romance categories. In 2014, her mystery novel *Point of Betrayal*, was awarded a Goldie as Best Mystery by the Golden Crown Literary Society (GCLS). Ann is also the proud recipient of the Alice B. Medal for her body of work. Her twenty-first novel, *The Convincing Hour*, her first YA novel, will be released in September, 2021.

Riley Scott

In addition to having published poetry and short stories, Riley Scott has worked as a grant and press writer and a marketing professional. She holds a degree in journalism. Riley's love for fiction began at a young age, and she has been penning stories for over a decade. Her days and her writing alike are fueled by strong coffee, humor, people watching, and just enough daydreaming to craft imaginative novels. She lives in Pensacola, Florida, with the love of her life and their four beloved dogs.

Laina Villeneuve

Laina Villeneuve lives in Southern California with her wife and three children. She consumes words. Mountains of words in the essays her college students write are her protein. Nonfiction reading is great fiber, and general fiction her fruits and veggies.

Lesbian romance is always dessert! You can feed her your comments at lainavilleneuve@gmail.com.

Blythe H. Warren

Blythe H. Warren survived fifteen years as a college English teacher before calling it quits. Now she has a much less stressful career in retail. Her first novel was a Lammy finalist, she won a Goldie for her second novel, *Bait and Switch*, and she writes the Matilda Smithwick mysteries under her real name (E.J. Cochrane). When she's not working or writing, she's training for her next marathon (which she always swears will be her last one). She and her partner live with their ball-obsessed pit bull, Gonzo, and his adoring feline fan club: Beatrix, Juniper and Aoife.

Bella Books, Inc.

Women. Books. Even Better Together.

P.O. Box 10543
Tallahassee, FL 32302

Phone: 800-729-4992
www.bellabooks.com

CPSIA information can be obtained
at www.ICGtesting.com
Printed in the USA
JSHW030153030721
16552JS00001B/30